LOST GIRL

LEIA STONE

Bloom books

Published by Bloom Books, an imprint of Sourcebooks
P.O. Box 4410, Naperville, Illinois 60567-4410
(630) 961-3900
sourcebooks.com

Originally self-published in 2021 by Leia Stone LLC.

Cataloging-in-Publication data is on file with the Library of Congress.

Printed and bound in the United States of America.
KP 10 9 8 7 6 5 4 3 2 1

*For my husband, who is my Sawyer. I love you babe...
even though we both turned out to be alphas.*

CHAPTER ONE

I CAME TO WITH A SPLITTING HEADACHE, PAIN THROB-
bing behind my eyelids so strongly that I whimpered.

'Demi! Fucking answer me!' Sawyer's angry voice
screamed in my head and I grabbed my temples in agony.

My eyes snapped open as the memory of everything
came crashing down on me. I kissed that other guy...
thinking it was Sawyer...and then he announced he was
taking Meredith as his new wife!

He didn't believe me...and then the vampires
kidnapped me.

Oh God.

The necklace. He'd been wearing some kind of ugly-
ass necklace that was no doubt magically affecting him.

I peered around the room to find that I was lying on
a cold concrete floor. There was a water bowl, like you
would set out for a dog...and that was it. The room was

tiny, more like a jail cell, but with a normal door and handle. The walls were plaster and I wondered if I could somehow peel at the plaster and break through into the next room or the outside. My eyes flicked down to the cuffs at my wrists and I whimpered again.

'Demi! Enough with this shit. Where are you?' Sawyer thundered again in my head and tears filled my eyes.

'Fuck you,' I managed to send before the cuffs sent an electrical jolt up my arms, causing me to cry out in pain.

Talking to Sawyer mentally must use magic, and that triggered the cuffs to hurt me.

Great.

'Demi!' Sawyer's voice threaded with annoyance at hearing my reply. *'Where are you? I've got half the damn campus looking for you. Eugene says he lost you and—'*

'Fuck you,' I said again, and the pain shot up my arms for a second time, but this time I clenched my teeth and pushed through the discomfort. My current anger at Sawyer was making this pain bearable. It was nothing compared to the ache in my heart.

I felt him bristle; we were tied together emotionally through the imprint, and it was hard to tease his emotions from my own.

'Demi. Why do I feel pain from you? Where. Are. You?'

What the hell did he care? He chose Meredith. Magical necklace or not.

That motherfucker.

I sighed, realizing he was my only link to the outside world. *'Vampire City, I think. Kidnapped. Can't talk much. Cuffed. Electric,'* I sent back as shock after shock ripped through me and into him.

'No!' he screamed, before I felt a possessive surge overcome me. My wolf bristled as Sawyer's alpha presence overwhelmed us both. It was as if he was trying to jump through our imprint and join me here.

'I thought you were lying about the vampires...' he said, his voice devoid of emotion. His actual emotions were something else completely.

Something wasn't right with him. He felt off, as if anytime he had a normal emotion it was tamped down. I had nothing to say to that so I stayed silent, deciding to sit up and have a look around. How long was I out? Were there drugs in the water? I didn't want to drink from the bowl like a dog; it seemed like an interrogation tactic to make me feel less human. But I *was* thirsty. I scanned the ceiling and then the air vent, zeroing in on a tiny red blinking light.

Camera.

I peered right at it and gave whoever was watching the middle finger.

'I'm coming for you,' Sawyer said, but I ignored him.

Fuck him. Fuck everyone right now.

The clickity clack of footsteps echoed down the hall and I bristled. Maybe the middle finger was a bad idea.

Before I had time to prepare, the door burst open and two men in lab coats entered with Queen Drake.

I froze upon seeing Vicon's mother. After what he did to me, and knowing she was trying to get Sawyer arrested for his murder, it made fresh, hot rage surge inside of me. Her black hair was pulled into a tight, high bun, and she wore a white silk blouse that nearly matched the color of her skin.

"What do we know?" she asked the man in the white lab coat, ignoring me as I stood, fisting my hands together and preparing to fight them. I might only be a useless human with these cuffs on, but I was a decent fighter and I wouldn't die without at least breaking her nose.

"Lie back down!" the second vampire in a lab coat said to me, producing a long stick with two blue glowing wires at the end.

Hmm, that looked a lot like—

He shoved the prod into my stomach and I fell to my knees screaming as searing pain jolted my entire body. My teeth clacked shut so hard I thought they would break.

'*Demi!*' Sawyer cried out, having probably felt that through our bond.

Queen Drake looked at me like I was a nuisance, like my scream was too loud for her perfect ears.

"I'm hypothesizing that we need to take off the cuffs in order to bottle her power," the first lab coat dude told her and showed her a tablet screen.

Bottle her power.

He said *bottle*...in relation to *me*.

A sickness rolled into me as I started to glean why they might have kidnapped me. I thought it was in retaliation to Vicon's murder, but no...they knew what I was and they meant to...bottle my power?

Oh hell no.

I jumped up, lunging for them both, when the second lab coat guy met me halfway, shoving the electric stick right into my chest.

The prods pricked my skin and my heart squeezed like it might burst; blackness danced in my vision, pain shaking me like nothing I'd ever felt before. Wetness pooled between my legs and I blinked, realizing I'd peed my pants.

How did I get on the floor? Where were the lab coats and the queen? I must have blacked out...? I looked down to see a red dot on the inside of my arm, like they'd taken blood from me.

No.

A sob burst from my chest as I realized how incredibly screwed I was.

'Demi...' Sawyer's voice was much softer this time. '*What happened? You went dark. Where are you? In a building? A house?*'

The absolute heartbreak of Sawyer choosing Meredith over me, of him not trusting me, it all came down on me like a pile of bricks, crushing my soul.

5

'You didn't believe me. How could you not believe me!' I whimpered as the pain from the cuffs lit up my arms. 'Take off that fucking necklace, Sawyer. It's spelled.'

'I have eyes! You kissed another dude. What was I supposed to think?' he shot back.

'You were supposed to trust me.' I didn't even feel the pain anymore, I was numb. 'Take off the necklace,' I whimpered, repeating myself.

'I'm coming for you,' he repeated. 'I'm not going to let anything happen to you. I…still love you.'

I scoffed at that. 'But you'll marry Meredith?'

Silence.

'I have to protect my family,' he said finally, and the pain in my heart somehow got more intense. 'And Meredith loves me,' he added, sounding confused.

'Take off the necklace, Sawyer!' I shouted, crying at the pain that talking to him was causing me.

'No. Meredith gave it to me. It was a special present.' He sounded like Sméagol protecting the one ring.

'You don't love me.' I spoke it like the fact it was.

'Yes I do.'

'This isn't love, Sawyer! Love and trust go together. That guy I kissed was you. He looked and talked like you. I was tricked, and someone who loved me would believe me.' I could smell burning hair and skin from the cuffs as they singed my arms. And I wept as this current hell became reality.

Silence.

'*I want to believe you…*' he said. '*I'm…confused. I feel…off.*'

That fucking necklace was a love spell. I just knew it. This wasn't him. This wasn't my Sawyer.

'Get Sage. *Show her the necklace Meredith got you,*' I whimpered as black dots danced at the edges of my vision. Maybe someone with some sense would rip that fucking thing off him.

'*If I kissed Meredith, and then you caught me, and I said I thought it was you, would you believe me?*' he growled, ignoring my comment about the necklace.

'*That's different, you're dating Meredith, you're dating half the goddamn school, Sawyer!*' A cry ripped from my throat and the pain became too much.

'*I never touched any of them,*' Sawyer growled. '*Ask around, I didn't kiss a single girl since I met you that day at Delphi.*'

My heart couldn't possibly break any more, but it did. I realized in this moment that the bone-crushing heartache I felt was part his. Through the bond, his heartache and mine had merged into a single beast that felt like it would kill us both.

'*You think I would kiss some rando knowing you were right outside? How stupid do you think I am? Take off that necklace. It's spelled, you idiot!*' The cuffs were so hot, I half wondered if they would catch fire and burn me alive.

His pain and agony laced through our bond, wrapping around me like a snake.

'Demi, I spoke to the high priestess of the Witch Lands. She says there is no magic that could make another look like me.'

My heart fell at those words.

'Then she's lying!'

Silence. I was in too much pain, holding on to too much anger to deal with any of this anymore.

'When I free you, we can talk more about it, but—'

'But nothing,' I whimpered. 'Your family curse has fucked you up. You're broken and you don't know how to trust people. It's not my job to convince you of something I didn't do wrong. If you can't trust me... it's over.'

'Demi, wait—'

'No,' I whimpered. 'In what reality would you ever be this mean to me, Sawyer? Think about it. Your necklace from Meredith is spelled and you're a fucking asshole. Goodbye.'

I couldn't deal with spelled-necklace-Sawyer anymore. I tore myself away from our bond so fast that I felt something fracture inside of me. A headache slammed into me at the same time the cuffs ripped so much electricity through me that everything went black again.

———•·•———

When I regained consciousness a second time, I was strapped onto a gurney. Bright lights blasted in my face as muffled voices faded in and out of consciousness.

Queen Drake's voice filled my ears. "Jesus, why does she look half-dead?"

A sharp male voice answered: "Looks like she tried to use her power too much. The cuffs reacted in doing their job."

"She's a fighter. That bodes well for the potency of the elixir transfer, right?" Her voice was smooth yet terrifying.

"Yes and no," the male voice said. "It seems the full potent magic we need to harvest from her will only come out with the cuffs off. I've tried everything else on her and it's like trying to tap power from a human."

She clucked her tongue. "Then we run the risk of battling her full powers."

"That's right, My Queen," he answered. I couldn't see their faces; they were blobs of darkness as the blinding light overwhelmed my vision.

"Well, that's fine, I can get a team of soldiers—"

"My liege," he interrupted. "Even with a full contingent of soldiers—"

"Did you just interrupt me?" she hissed as the bright light over my face suddenly went dark and a body flew across the room, taking the lamp with him. A noise crashed to my left as his body hit the wall.

Holy shit.

I was grateful for the reprieve from the brain-numbing light until the queen peered over me, saliva glistening on her teeth. A shriek tore from my throat when I saw the bleeding heart in her hand, crimson blood trickling down her fingers. In the dim light I peered at the guy she'd thrown across the room. An open cavity lay in the center of his chest as his body slowly decomposed to ash.

"I wonder what she tastes like raw?" the queen queried to someone else in the room, and my gaze snapped back to her.

Holy fuck.

I could *feel* the evil coming off this woman as fear melted out of my chest and settled into my limbs. Her bun was so tight that it pulled the corners of her eyes up, making it look like she'd had a facelift. But her eyes; they were as black as her soul and held no life.

"I'm sure one feeding wouldn't jeopardize the project," a second man said from behind her.

That got me moving. I bucked against the straps that held me to the table, fur running down my arms as my wolf tried to be free. Pain shot up my arms as the cuffs engaged and the queen laughed, a high shrill sound.

Before she could step any closer, the door at the far wall burst open and a man wearing black army fatigues skidded to a stop at the foot of my gurney. He was barely winded, but his cheeks were slightly flushed, which was saying something for a bloodsucker who was dead.

10

"What is it?" the queen growled at him, never taking her eyes off the pulse at my neck.

"Werewolves. West gate. They're asking for the girl," he responded, and my heart suddenly grew wings.

He came for me. That fucking asshole, who I was so pissed at I could punch him in the balls, came for me. I'd torn our bond; I couldn't really feel him like I could before. Only if I dug really deep and searched for him inside of me did I feel his essence. His strong, loving, and fragile soul was linked to my strong, guarded, and broken one.

'Demi!' Sawyer shouted suddenly in my mind as if he felt me searching for him. *'Oh my God, Sage ripped off the necklace and then punched me in the face. I'm so fucking sorry. It was a spell. Please forgive me.'*

A tear slid down my cheek at the relief that Sage had gotten that freaking thing off him, but I was in such shit right now it didn't matter.

"Fuck," the queen said at the guard who had spoken, and then pointed at a man in a lab coat. "Get me that elixir, and if she dies during the extraction process, throw her body in a wood chipper. I can't be caught being involved in this. I have the Magical Creatures Council on my ass enough as it is."

"Yes, my lady." He bowed to her as my stomach sank.

Throw her body in a wood chipper? Say what?

I screamed as I bucked against the restraints and she

11

lunged for me. At the same time I felt something snap. Not the binds or anything physical—something inside of me. But it wasn't me... It was *Sawyer*. His alpha power washed over me, filled me up. I pulled on the bindings once more and was rewarded with the satisfying crack of metal as the hinge gave way.

He lent me his power... It was a fleeting thought before I lurched from the gurney and headbutted the queen of the vampires before she could attack me.

Pain exploded between my eyebrows as my forehead smashed into her nose and she hissed.

Dizzy and stiff, I launched from the table only to trip and fall to the floor. My ankles were bound. I splayed out my hands to catch the brunt of my fall, and then rushed into a standing position as quickly as possible. With another burst of Sawyer's energy, I kicked out and snapped the chain holding my legs together.

"That bitch broke my nose!" the queen roared as I made it to the open doorway at the back of the room. I was just about to reach the hallway when a million volts of electricity slammed into my back.

No.

A wail ripped from my throat as pain laced across my skin, causing it to burn and tighten. My whole body shook as agony encompassed me. Falling to my knees, I barely had time to get in another breath before a knee crashed into my face, hitting me right in the eye socket.

Sharp pain exploded in my brain and then my lip as the queen crashed down on me with powerful fast blows, one after another.

"The wolves have reached the main castle, my lady," a male voice said, and she stopped immediately, freezing with her fist in the air.

When I looked up into her dead black eyes, I understood how Vicon was able to easily do what he did to me. I mean, if he was raised by this demon, then I expected nothing less of him. If this was his role model for how to treat a woman, then I was no longer shocked he'd raped me with his friends.

"Drain her essence and bring it to me while I deal with the dogs," she snapped, and left the room.

I curled into a ball in the doorway, hurt, scared, and unsure what to do. Another man in a lab coat held the prod out, threatening me with another jolt that I wasn't sure I could take, especially not without rapid healing. I was all but human with these cuffs on.

"No. Please," I whimpered.

Two guards now glowered over me and I couldn't see a way out of this, not in my current shape. My wolf wanted to come forward, but I pushed her back. I couldn't take another jolt.

'Fight. Fight back.' It was a faint whisper, but I heard him.

Sawyer.

I didn't dare respond for fear of activating the cuffs,

but he clearly felt through our broken and tattered bond that I was in trouble.

"I can't," I whimpered aloud. "I'm done." A sob escaped me.

The man in the lab coat frowned at me. "Get her back on the table," he snapped to the guards.

The two vampire guards bent to hook their hands under my armpits when two things happened simultaneously.

1. A fire alarm went off.
2. Sawyer's alpha power surged so strongly through me that I felt his wolf nearly jump inside my body. The cuffs didn't activate though, so I breathed a sigh of relief.

Not questioning anything, I punched both of the guards in the throats simultaneously with precision. They fell to their knees coughing and I lunged out into the hallway, pumping my wobbly legs, still dangling a thin silver chain behind me. I turned right and ran as fast as I could while the fire alarm blared so loudly my head felt like it was going to explode. I hit a dead end and then turned left. The fire alarm ceased its blaring, and footsteps pounded behind me. Ducking into a room to catch my breath and think of a plan, I pulled the door closed behind me, panting.

This building must have been some type of science

building because I was now in an empty room with a stainless-steel table, filled with beakers and Petri dishes. Along the far wall was a giant windowpane overlooking a thick forest. There were machines I didn't recognize but it all looked very high-end. When my eyes fell on the maroon leather briefcase, I stilled.

It was the same one the vampires' lawyer had brought to the meeting and indicated it held Sawyer's DNA.

My heart hammered in my chest as I stepped forward. Footsteps thundered just outside the door and I froze.

"I don't smell her!" a male screamed.

"Because of the cuffs." I recognized Mr. Lab Coat's voice.

I crouched behind the stainless-steel table just as the door opened.

My heart leapt into my throat as I peered around for a weapon, but then to my surprise the door closed and the footsteps retreated.

Holy shifter, that was close.

Salty copper filled my mouth and I realized I was bleeding. Standing over the stainless-steel table, I caught my reflection and winced.

Black eye, split lip bleeding into my mouth, haunted eyes. It reminded me of the night of my attack and I just wanted to get the fuck out of here, but I also wanted to help Sawyer.

I still loved him, even though he chose someone else over me. I knew it had to have been the necklace.

Reaching out with shaky hands, I opened the brief-case and held my breath.

It was empty.

Oh God, no!

Searching the counter, I noticed what looked like some hair and pipette. Was that Sawyer's fur? The machine on the far wall was whirring and I wondered if it was some type of DNA extractor or whatever they were called. I didn't watch enough *CSI* for this shit. There was only one way to make sure Sawyer's fur never left this room.

Reaching out to one of the Bunsen burners, I grabbed the matches that sat right in front.

Sawyer's energy surged within me as I felt his presence wash over me.

'Run, Demi. There are too many of them. They are trying to keep me from searching for you without a warrant. Can you get out?'

Shit.

I couldn't respond to him. I couldn't take another jolt.

I spun on the gas and lit the match, igniting the flame of the Bunsen burner as I had dozens of times at Delphi High. After setting the lit Bunsen burner on the table, I turned and grabbed the metal chair nearest to me. I needed to make sure I had a way out of here before I blew the place up and destroyed Sawyer's DNA. Picking up the chair took every ounce of whatever strength I had left. This was one of those pretty view windows that didn't open, it was just for looks. Pulling the chair over my head, I chucked it hard at the windowpane and it crashed into it, caving it outward with the chair stuck in the glass.

Not ideal. Not like in the movies. Dammit.

It had made the loudest noise possible and I still had no exit. Pulling the chair out, I threw it again, sweating as it crashed into the glass and finally fell out the other side.

Crisp autumn air blew inside and I knew it was time to get the hell out of here. Grabbing two glass chemical bottles, I spun the lids off without even looking at the label and prayed they were flammable as all hell. If Sawyer's DNA was in this room, then I was going to incinerate it.

Stepping up to the edge of the window, I turned over my shoulder and chucked the bottles onto the flame, just as the door to the room opened. Kicking off the ground, I leapt out the window as an explosion rocked the building.

Heat and pressure pushed into my back, but I ignored it as the ground came up to meet me. Rolling into the fall, I crashed down on my right shoulder, which flared with pain as I heard a popping noise. But I knew I had not a moment to lose, and burst to my feet, running for the woods.

I didn't look behind me, I didn't even know where I was going, I just ran. My shoulder throbbed, my arm hanging limply at my side. I thought it was out of the socket but not broken. My head still pounded and the skin around my cuffs was bleeding, but I was alive.

'*Tell me you got out! I see smoke, Demi. Tell me you are fucking safe or I'll go wild!*' Sawyer roared in my mind and my headache intensified.

'Got...out,' I sent back as the cuffs' magic ignited, sending a burst of fresh electricity through my body. It was too much—I'd taken on too much. My skin felt raw and I sobbed, stumbling as I fell to my knees in the forest.

'*Run, Demi. Run until you reach a new territory. If you head west, I can meet you. If that's not possible, head east to the trolls. Don't go south or you will hit the Wild Lands and the Ithaki.*'

I managed to stand, trying to figure out where the fuck west was when I heard feet pounding on the forest floor far behind me.

I took off running like my ass was on fire, through the thick trees even though everything hurt, even though I wanted to fall down and give up. My injured arm flopped wildly around as I tried to pin it to my chest with my good hand. Tears streamed down my face because I had no idea where I was going. I was still mad at Sawyer for not believing me and choosing Meredith even though he wore a spelled necklace, and yet I wanted to run right into his arms.

My feet pounded the damp earth as I skipped over fallen logs and bushy ferns.

Run.

Run.

My inner wolf cheered me on. I ran blindly until I couldn't hear the footsteps behind me anymore and my legs burned. I started to stumble, unable to keep up any longer. How long had passed? An hour? It felt like ten. My chest heaved, lungs burning as exhaustion settled into me. Slowing, I felt relief wash over me when I saw the little red flags that demarcated a property line. Just beyond the flags was a small two-foot-tall bush hedge.

Please be the wolves. Please be wolf land! A sob ripped from my throat as I tasted my freedom.

Don't be the Wild Lands.

Don't be the trolls.

Please be the wolves.

I was on the ground now, sobbing and crawling with one usable arm as the fight left me.

Inch by inch, I neared the border and finally crawled over the red flag line, falling onto my back, looking up at the sky and wondering if I would die.

If I was going to die, then this wasn't a bad way to go. The sun was up, birds were chirping, and the trees rustled in the wind.

'God, please don't let me die.'

I went to church once with a human friend and it was actually a nice experience. The singing, the handshakes and hugs, everyone was so nice to me; I wasn't used to being accepted like that. I'd meant to send that prayer up to God as an internal thought, but I must have sent it to Sawyer because the cuffs jolted what was left of me. I had no more tears to cry, so dry sobs racked my body as Sawyer's energy bristled against me.

'No. No. No. Don't say that,' came his reply as his severed and broken soul bled into our fractured bond. 'I should have believed you. Even under a spell I should have known. Jesus, Demi, how will you ever forgive me? The necklace. You have to believe me, I...wasn't me.'

I sensed that he was distracted, and our bond wasn't the same after I'd torn myself away from it. He felt so far away. I was too weak to respond, but his grief was nearly choking me alive. I felt it even though it was distant and diluted, the internal shame and regret he was feeling bled into me.

'Demi, you're my true mate. I'm so gutted that I hurt you like that in front of everyone.' His voice cracked. 'Please tell me there's a chance you'll forgive me?'

Tears streamed down my face as I thought of the time we first made love, how tender he was, how he asked permission. How I didn't feel complete without him in my life, and I never would. This was Meredith's fault, and I knew from Raven that love spells were dangerous and all-consuming, sometimes driving the person who took them to go mad or commit suicide. I was just glad it was broken. I wanted to be in his arms again.

I risked one more shock to tell him something in case I really did die.

'Forgiven,' I huffed, and then yelped at the shocks that racked my body.

Relief rushed through our bond on his side. *'Just hang on. I'll find you. Wherever you are, I'll find you, Demi. Don't give up.'*

Blackness faded at the edges of my vision, and then a blur of brown hair flashed in front of my face.

"Sawyer?" I whimpered, looking up at the sky. Had he found me already?

A perplexed yet strikingly beautiful female troll looked down at me and grimaced.

No.

The trolls were in an alliance with the vampires. She'd hand me over for sure. I wasn't in Wolf City or the Wild Lands. I'd just landed myself square in troll territory, and with that I'd signed my own death warrant. The beautiful young woman pulled a shotgun from somewhere at her hip and held it firmly in two hands.

"Stop right there, bloodsucker," she growled, and my heart thundered in my chest. Looking above me, I saw a male vampire standing just at the edge of the red flags.

"She's ours," he hissed, and took a step forward.

She cocked the shotgun and he stopped.

Looking down at me with deep soulful eyes, she nodded her head to the vampire. "You with him?"

"No," I croaked with what little energy I had left. "Help me...please."

He lunged for me and the shotgun went off, sending a ringing sound throughout my ears. I flinched as a hole the size of a baseball appeared in his chest.

The troll leaned down and the smell of jasmine washed over me. "Your arm looks out of socket. Want me to reset it so you don't heal wrong?" she asked, her eyes still full of concern for me. Packard and the other troll assholes at Delphi were the only interaction I'd had with her kind. I wasn't prepared for her generosity.

I just nodded.

She stepped away for a minute and brought a wheelbarrow with her; there were a few ears of corn inside of it. "Get in. In case you pass out, I can bring you back to the house."

I tried to stand and swayed as she swooped in. "Poor thing. What did they do to you?" She clicked her tongue as she inspected my bleeding cuffs. I helped her as best I could, but it was painful to move. Dropping me slowly into the wheelbarrow, she inspected my arm, shaking her head as she squeezed the shoulder blade and I whimpered. Reaching out, she grabbed one of the pieces of corn and shoved it in my mouth.

"Ready?"

Fuck no.

I just nodded. Knowing that if this didn't set right and healed wrong, I could be permanently maimed. Good thing my cuffs kept that from happening anytime soon. She pressed her left hand on my shoulder and grabbed my elbow with her right. The mere act of grasping it lightly caused a whimper to rip from my throat.

"One," she said, and yanked so hard I screamed into the corn and bit down as blackness finally took me into its sweet embrace.

CHAPTER TWO

THE SOUND OF A WOMAN SOFTLY HUMMING FILTERED through my ears and into my brain.

"Rosedaaaaaale," she sang sweetly. "The place where flowers grooooow." Her voice was melodic and soothing, "Rosedale, the land of fertile groooound."

I popped my eyelids open and recognized the sweet troll woman from the border.

Pushing her singing out of my mind, I grasped for that bond that kept me in touch with Sawyer.

'Sawyer? I'm in Troll Village!' I tried and whimpered when the cuffs lit up my arms in excruciating pain, frying the tender skin there.

There was no reply and now that I focused on it...I felt...nothing. I couldn't feel him like I normally could. His essence, once so tightly woven to mine, was... severed.

The woman's singing cut off as she walked over to me, eyes wide in alarm. She'd tied my shoulder up in a leather sling and had laid me in a handmade cotton bed. Dark, rough logs were stacked high to make the walls; packed dry mud filled the gaps. A kerosene lamp hanging on a hook illuminated the polished dark wood floor, and everything from the muted woven rug to the carved nightstand looked handmade. It was simple yet clean and homely. I was lying on a makeshift mattress in the corner of an open living room. The fireplace at the far wall held a pot inside as orange flames licked at the edges.

"You thirsty?" The woman came over, carrying a stainless-steel cup of water.

At the mere mention of water, my tongue felt swollen and dry. She held the cup to my lips and I chugged half the thing in one swallow.

"Thank you," I panted as she reached underneath me and heaved me into a sitting position, resting my back against the wall and shoving a pillow under it to make me comfortable.

The jasmine flower she wore behind her ear caused the scent to wash over me. I noticed she looked about my age, maybe a year or two older. When she pulled back to hand me some more water, I laced my fingers over hers and stilled the cup mid-air. "Thank you. You saved my life." My voice cracked and she nodded. Even for being in her early twenties, there was a hardness to her. She was beautiful, but tough times had not left her unmarred. My gaze ran over her soft caramel skin to the two tiny tusks that protruded out of her cheeks. Her honey-brown eyes were almond shaped and her thick, silky hair made me envious. I never thought I would think a troll was beautiful, but she was.

"They're monsters," she said, and something dark flashed across her face. I wondered if she'd had a personal run in with a vampire, one like mine. "And us women gotta stick together."

That brought a smile to my lips. No matter our race or differences, she only saw the commonality. "What's your name?" I asked, taking the water and helping myself to another mouthful as she fussed about me, checking my shoulder injury.

She smiled. "Marmal."

"I'm Demi." I used my left hand to grasp my right injured elbow in a typical troll gesture of being well-met that I'd learned from Delphi, and her smile grew wider.

She grasped her elbow and bowed her head. "Well met, Demi. How did you learn our greeting?"

I sighed. "Delphi…" I wasn't sure if she would know what that was, but she winced the moment I said it, so that told me she did.

"Banished? Is that where you got those?" She pointed to my wrists.

I nodded. "Sort of. Wore them all my life, but these are new. Vampires."

Again that vicious predatorial look was back. "I tried to take them off while you were out. They shocked me!" she spat.

"Magic. Keeps me from shifting." Again I felt for Sawyer and again got nothing.

No. No. No. What did that mean? Was it this place, being in Troll Village? Or were we simply too far away from each other? I'd done something in my anger. I'd severed our imprint and it was barely working before, and now it felt completely busted.

I wanted to cry, but Marmal pulled me from my panicked thoughts.

A frown pulled at her lips. "Are you running from Werewolf City? You can stay here a few days, but the vampires will probably speak to the Troll Council and they'll come looking for you eventually and turn you in."

That was the last thing I wanted. "I'm actually trying to get back to Wolf City. The vampires kidnapped me. Do you know a way?"

She frowned. "The closest way to Wolf City from here is through the Wild Lands, Vampire City...or all the way around."

I frowned. "All the way around what? I didn't grow up here."

Vampire City and Wild Lands were out of the question.

She nodded and stood, walking across the room. She went to a little wooden desk and pulled out a piece of

27

old suede. "Here, you can have this extra map I made for my little sister. She's married off now."

Married off? I knew nothing about troll culture. "And you're not?" I grasped the map and started to unroll it.

She chuckled. "Men don't want to marry me. I'm a successful farmer with my own land, no debt, and a brain between my ears."

I grinned, instantly liking her. "Parents?" I asked, holding the map flat on my lap.

"Died when I was fifteen. I've been on my own ever since."

I frowned. So young, and with a little sister to take care of…that was tragic. No wonder she was so capable; it was her only option.

"I'm sorry to hear that," I told her. I peered down at the map in my lap and my heart sank.

"So…this is a map of Magic City?" I traced my finger along the path I would have to take to get to our nearest ally, the light fey. It was sandwiched between the Dark Fey Territory and the Witch Lands, which touched Werewolf City. That meant I would have to travel through all of Troll Village, and then through the entirety of the Dark Fey Territory to reach the light fey. It was either that or risk going back into Vampire City which wasn't an option. The Wild Lands also weren't an option, not after Sawyer killed Butcher. They'd skin me alive on the spot.

"It's not ideal," she sighed, "but I can give you one of my donkeys and a traveling pack…"

That was a very kind offer and a good backup plan. "Thank you. That would be great…but if I could just call my friend and tell him exactly where I am, he will send a helicopter to get me before the vampires even realize." I knew my mom, Raven, and my dad's number by heart. One of them could call Sawyer, because I hadn't memorized his.

She looked confused, and then understanding crossed her features and she nodded. "You mean a telephone? Oh, we don't have electronics in Troll Village. We believe they are cursed and will steal our magic."

My heart dropped.

Of course not. And my cell phone and backpack were MIA since my kidnapping.

Fuck.

"So…I'll take that donkey and travel pack, then." I gave her a weak smile as my heart grew more worried. Ride a donkey through the dark fey territories and get to Light Fey City to find a phone and call my parents?

Easy peasy. I totally got this.

Just kidding, this was clearly how I die.

She pointed to my cuffs. "Those will get you spotted quicker. I can't take them off, but I can cover them."

She pulled some thick leather from a box under the sofa next to the bed and started to wrap them around the cuffs, measuring. "Stay the night and you can leave at first light. You don't want to cross these woods after dark. Walk in the day posing as a trader and sleep high in the treetops at night."

I gulped, nodding. Walk in the day, sleep high in a tree at night. Got it. "Trading what? Won't they smell my wolf?"

She nodded. "They'll think you're Ithaki or Paladin, not a city wolf and not banished. The Paladin wolves often trade furs and bone blades at our market."

They did?

I didn't know that. I wondered if my biological father, Run, had done that.

"Okay." I questioned this plan but was grateful for her help.

"I'll give you a few items to trade if you get caught, but you'll have to travel all day to make good time."

My eyes widened as I became more and more afraid of this plan.

"Got a motorcycle or something?" I gave a nervous laugh and she looked confused again. "It's like a metal donkey that goes really fast," I told her.

She clicked her teeth. "Demon technology." She tapped my cuff. "See where that got you?"

Maybe she had a point, but I missed my iPhone right about now and the connection it gave me to the outside world. Okay, my boyfriend just broke out of an evil love spell, I was trapped in Troll Village, and I needed to travel through Dark Fey Territory to get to the Prime

Minister of Light Fey City...an ally who'd sniffed me and moaned. This was fine.

Everything was fine.

She motioned to my jeans and T-shirt. "Traders don't dress like that. I'll give you clothes too."

I sighed. "I don't have anything to pay you with, but I can—"

She grabbed my hand and held it, her eyes swimming with emotion. "A year after my mom died...the vampires paid me monthly visits." All vulnerability fled when her eyes creased to slits of absolute hatred. My stomach dropped at her words. "At first, I was just glad they left my little sister alone, but then my old neighbor, Timatu, dropped by and saw what was going on... He taught me how to fight back."

I squeezed her hand to show support and she nodded, wiping at a stray tear.

"I killed my first bloodsucker that summer, and then another, and another, until they learned to stop coming or they'd keep dying." She flicked her eyes to the wall behind me and I turned to see a rack full of shotguns, silver stakes, a sickle, and other vampire-killing weapons.

Holy shit, homegirl was a killing machine, because she had to be. I understood what she was telling me. That even though I had nothing to give her, getting me away from the vampires was enough payment for her.

"I'm so sorry. Something similar happened to me," I told her.

She nodded. "So I don't want payment. I want to pay it forward and help you, like my neighbor helped me."

My throat constricted with emotion. Gifts that were given with no expectation of return were the best kind. "Thank you. I won't forget this kindness."

She nodded and released my hand. "See if you can walk. You seem to have taken a beating and I want to make sure you are strong enough. Bathhouse is just off the porch if you want to wash up."

And with that, Marmal and I became temporary roommates. I shuffled outside and took a shower in her bathhouse, putting on some handmade cotton clothing she left for me, careful to baby my injured shoulder. It was black and blue, like my eye. I looked pretty beat up, but Marmal had an arnica salve for my eye and a minty rub that I put on my shoulder that lessened the pain.

When I stepped into the kitchen, she called me right over to the stove and taught me how to make *pag'al*. It was like a sweet puffy bread that was delicious with butter. I also tried goat's milk for the first time, and even some stewed rabbit. As long as I mentally told myself it was chicken, it tasted great.

Later that night, after helping her clean up, I wished her goodnight and then lay awake for a long time in bed. I wondered what Sawyer was doing right now. Was he still looking for me? Did he still love me? Did he still love Meredith? Raven once told me that love potions only worked if the person genuinely had feelings for another person. It could amp those feelings up but not create them out of nothing.

I didn't know what to think about that, so I stared at the weapons wall of the house until sleep took me.

———·—·———

I was awoken by the crisp, clear sound of Marmal singing. She had a lovely voice. Even though life had been hard on her, it hadn't dampened her joy.

"Rise and shine." She stepped over to me with a plate of steaming-hot boiled eggs that didn't look like they came from a chicken, and some shredded meat over purple potatoes piled high upon the plate.

"Freshen up quickly and then join me for breakfast. I have some things to tell you," she said, and then set the plate on the table.

I quickly went to the bathhouse and used some of this clay mint teeth brushing powder she'd given me with a handmade toothbrush. I reapplied the healing salves, taking care to try to get under my cuffs with the arnica. My forearms were the most beat up from the constant shocks. I was grateful to see I looked less banged-up today. My split lip was healing; a thick, almost black scab in a line ran down the bottom. By the time I was done, only about ten minutes had passed and I raced back to the house eager to get on my way before I chickened out or vampires showed up.

Marmal was waiting for me; two wicker baskets lay over the top of our food to keep the steam in.

"Thank you," I told her as we pulled off our baskets and started to eat. "What do you have to tell me?"

A slow grin pulled across her face. "You seem to have caught the eye of the werewolf alpha's son."

My heart thundered in my chest. "What do you mean?"

She took a drink from her stainless-steel cup and then leveled her eyes at me. "Because we don't use technology, we trolls don't have much in the way of entertainment. So gossip is much loved in our culture."

Get on with it, woman.

"What did you hear?"

She nodded. "I went over to Larada's farm early this morning to trade a few things and she said that rumor is..." She leaned forward for affect. "...that the alpha's son has gone mad searching for his mate who was taken by the vampires."

Gone mad? I hoped that was a cultural barrier and I wasn't interpreting that literally.

I sighed in relief. He was still looking for me, that was good. "What else did she say?"

Marmal pulled her long brown hair over one shoulder and away from her food. "That he was sending out delegates to each sector to negotiate your return, and there is a million-dollar reward if you are delivered home safely."

I swooned a little at that, unable to fight the grin that swept across my face. Thank God Sage pulled that necklace off of him; he sounded like his old self again. But why couldn't I hear him through our bond?

"But then the vampires said they would pay two million." Her fork stilled at her mouth.

I swallowed hard, trying to read her face. A two-million-dollar bounty on my head by the vampires was *not* good.

"I lied," Marmal said suddenly. "I *do* want payment for helping you."

My stomach sank. Two million dollars for turning me into the vampires was a lot of money. She could—

"Pay me in gossip." She grinned, popping a potato into her mouth. "Tell. Me. Everything about the alpha's son and how he became so fond of you." Her eyes lit up and a deep relief rushed through my body.

Gossip was all she wanted? That I could do.

"It all started one morning at Delphi University..." I said, and then proceeded to tell her my entire story with Sawyer. I left out parts like my being a split shifter and found other things to put in its place that would make sense. I didn't realize, until recounting this story, how many times Sawyer protected me, fought for me, saved me.

By the time I was done, I was left feeling empty without him here, not knowing what was going on with Meredith or any of that. Did he blame her for the necklace or simply let her off the hook? Was he still marrying her because she was a safe bet for his family curse? I had so many questions and zero answers.

Marmal looked feral by the time I'd finished the story. "When you get back, you should hike Meredith right up Waterfall Mountain and push her over the other side!" Marmal declared, slamming her fork onto her empty plate.

I chuckled. Wouldn't that be nice. "Her mom is some bigwig in werewolf society. He probably slapped her on the wrist."

She shook her head and sighed, then looked at my empty plate. "All right, let's get you off. Remember you need to travel by day and sleep high in the trees at night." She stood and took our plates to the sink.

I nodded, but suddenly felt scared. Why couldn't she go with me? See me across to the Dark Fey Territory? She must have read my mind.

"I wish I could escort you, but it's a two-day journey to the border and then another two days back for me. Four days is too long to leave the animals on my farm. And all of my neighbors have their own work to do."

I nodded, completely understanding. "I'll be fine."

Travel across Troll Village on a donkey, what could go wrong? I sifted through my memories of Packard telling stories of his childhood growing up. Weren't there dark forest creatures that hunted at night? Or was that in the fey lands?

I swallowed hard and followed Marmal outside into the morning light. We crossed the large front yard and then stepped over to the big barn.

"This is Ginny." She smoothed a hand over the donkey's grayish fur and the animal nuzzled into her. "She's trained to come home on her own, so just let her loose when you get to the dark fey border."

I nodded, wondering how an animal could travel back that far without guidance, but kept it to myself. Maybe it was magic. The trolls had a way with animals.

"This food pouch hangs from her neck, so she will self-feed. It's got enough for the journey and some extra if you get into trouble." She indicated a leather sack that hung around the animal's neck. It was full of some kind of pellet or grain.

I nodded again, growing more and more nervous by the moment.

Heaving a large leather sack over one shoulder, Marmal began to tie it to the animal's backside, showing me how to loosen and retighten the straps. "Shelf stable food for two weeks, water for three days. Running water is safe to drink, standing water is bad. Got it?"

Fuck.

"Sure."

Maybe I could just go back to Vampire City and Sawyer could negotiate my return?

Yeah right.

Flashes of them talking about "bottling" my essence flooded my mind and I shivered.

Next, Marmal stepped over to the exterior barn wall and pulled a shotgun from where it was leaning against the side. "You know how to shoot one of these?"

My eyes widened and I shook my head.

She nodded, breaking the barrel in half to expose two dark holes. "Pop two shells in here…" She snapped the gun shut. "Close it, aim, pull back hammers, and shoot."

I gave her a dry smile. "Is that all?"

She grinned. "It'll have some kick, so prop it on your shoulder. It's your last resort weapon, because you can hear it a mile away."

I nodded. Pop, close, aim, pull hammers, shoot. Last resort. "Got it."

She handed me two leather cuffs that fit perfectly over my metal ones to disguise them, and I pulled her in for an unexpected hug. "Thank you," I croaked.

This woman had quite literally saved my life when all I'd expected of her was to turn me in. It showed me that not all trolls were bad, just like not all Paladin were bad.

Her jasmine scent washed over me and she squeezed me back. If we didn't live worlds apart, we would be good friends, I just knew it.

"Be safe. You're a Paladin wolf trader, remember?" She pulled back as I slipped the leather cuffs over my metal ones. They were hard like they were wrapped over plastic or something to help it keep shape, perfectly fitting over mine and covering them completely. I looked like a badass archer and not a girl on the run from banishment.

"Be careful, Demi. When you make it back, if you send word to Marmal at Rosedale, rumor will reach me and I'll know you are safe."

Both of our eyes were glistening. We were two women who had bonded over hard times, and it was tough to say goodbye. I couldn't reach Sawyer, I was all alone, and if the vampires weren't after me I would just stay here for a while with her and learn to cook and tend to the animals. It was peaceful here.

"Go on!" She waved me off and wiped her eyes. "I can't be seen crying, I have a reputation to uphold," she joked with a smile.

I nodded, not trusting myself to speak, and then hopped onto Ginny. Reaching back behind me, I slipped the shotgun between the straps of my pack for easy access. Then I pulled out the oil-stained map Marmal had given me and pointed Ginny in the direction of the Dark Fey Territory.

"Goodbye, Marmal. I'll send word." I waved to her.

She nodded, swallowing hard, and waved me off with glistening, teary eyes.

Part of me wanted to stay longer. Life was easy and joyous here on the farm with her, but I knew I needed to get back. I needed to see Sawyer. I needed to kick Meredith's ass. And most importantly, I needed to find out more about what the vampires wanted with me, what this *bottling of my essence* was all about.

———————

I passed a few farmers who waved or greeted me, asking what I had to trade. Marmal had given me a few less-than-desirable items so that I could just be on my way. And people did decline quickly. It seemed a Paladin trader was a regular fixture here in Troll Village. I wondered just how bad they could be if the only one I ever met had saved my life, and if my mother loved one. Maybe Sawyer was wrong about them.

Obviously he was.

The day went by painfully slow. No TV, no social media, and no one to even talk to. I found myself having made-up conversations in my head. A conversation with Sawyer, another with Meredith, with Sage, and even Eugene. I felt like I was going crazy by nightfall. I didn't stop to eat, just shoved bits of dried berries or nuts in my mouth as Ginny walked, and only took a rest if she seemed like she needed it.

Now that darkness was creeping in the forest, I decided to climb a tree like Marmal said and attempt to sleep. It wasn't until I looked up that I noticed there were actual little platforms every hundred or so feet. Sitting in the treetops was a wooden bed...it must be a normal fixture in troll society, like a free hotel or something.

Careening Ginny over to one of the platform bed trees, I tied her to the bottom and poured some of my water in a dish, giving it to her. "You did good today." I patted her as she sucked water through her pursed lips and ate from her food pouch. Next, I shouldered my pack and my shotgun and started the task of climbing the tree.

This is so much easier when you're five years old.

With my injured shoulder, climbing was near impossible. My foot slipped a few times and I almost dropped the shotgun twice. When I finally made it to the top, my right arm was quaking with fatigue; exhaustion bled from my limbs as I stretched onto the flat, hard wooden sky bed. My thighs and ass were sore from riding the donkey all day and flexing constantly to counterbalance myself. I couldn't imagine how she must feel carrying my weight all day.

Through the trees, I watched the sky slowly darken above me. How the hell had I gotten to this moment? My brain struggled to comprehend how I was lying in a treetop in Troll Village when two nights ago I'd been getting ready to meet Sawyer and have him announce I was the one he was picking. I sighed, pulling the thin suede blanket over me that Marmal had packed. Fatigue and pain burned in my limbs, and even though it was probably only like 7 p.m., I was ready for sleep.

There was one thing I wanted to do first though. I knew he was probably desperately worried about me and I wasn't sure if I broke our bond or if we were too far away or what, and even though it would hurt, I had to try.

'*Sawyer...?*' I whispered, flinching as the hot wires shot electricity up my barely healing arms. I waited, stilling my thoughts and hoping for anything. A word, a feeling, a sign...

I must have lain there an hour waiting for Sawyer to respond. At some point when the darkness hit, I heard hoof beats and yips and growls. Like a pack of wild hyena's was down there feeding on something. Now I understood why trolls slept in the trees... I tried to stay awake, in case whatever animals were down there could climb, or if Ginny needed me, but my limbs felt too heavy and finally sleep took me.

CHAPTER THREE

A SNAPPING TWIG JOLTED ME AWAKE, HEART HAMMER-ing in my chest. The sky was pitch dark and the moon was high in the sky, but that sound... I reached for the shotgun, only to feel it wasn't there.

Fuck.

When I heard it cock, my heart plunged into my stomach. I sprang up into a crouched position, but before I could turn around, the cold steel barrel pressed into the back of my neck.

"Who are you?" There was a slight accent to the man's voice, and I swallowed hard, trying to rein in my fear.

"My name is Mara," I said quickly, taking Marmal's name and shortening it. If there was a two-million-dollar vampire bounty on my head, I sure as hell wasn't saying I was Demi.

"*Who* are you, wolf?" His voice was scratchy and laced with anger.

"I'm...Mara. A Paladin trader—"

The gun shoved deeper into my neck and I stopped talking.

"You're no Paladin, I *know* my people," he hissed. "They don't have hair the color of corn silk."

Oh shit.

What were the odds I would run into an *actual* Paladin wolf trader out here? Why did the universe hate me?

I chose my next words carefully. "I'm a banished city wolf on the run."

The butt of the gun eased off the back of my neck and I took that as a good sign. Raising my arms, I showed him my leather wrist cuffs. "These hide my shackles. I'm just trying to get to Light Fey City."

He pulled the gun completely away from my neck and then the wood creaked as he stepped out in front of me.

Whoa.

Dude, put some pants on. He was nearly naked but for a suede crotch cloth, his muscles as lean and chiseled as a fucking statue. Brown, tanned skin ran the length of his body up to his chocolate brown hair. But it was his eyes that stunned me. His eyes were almond shaped and blue—the same color blue as the man who'd saved me when I fell down the mountain.

"You...look like him," I breathed, and his whole body flinched.

His grip on the gun tightened and he crouched before me, two streaks of dark blue war paint on his cheeks.

"Who?"

Shit. I shouldn't have said anything, but I wondered if he could smell a lie or something, so I decided honesty was best.

I swallowed hard. "The man who saved me when I fell down Waterfall Mountain a few weeks ago."

His entire face fell, and I saw grief bleed into his beautiful features. This guy couldn't be but a year older than me, yet he looked so old right now, like he carried decades of stress and sadness.

"What happened?" His voice was sharp but forgiving as his fingers went slack over the gun. "We only found the body and assumed Ithaki."

I swallowed, my own eyes getting teary as I realized the man who'd saved me probably had a family, maybe even this kid, and I'd done nothing to try and find them, to tell them what happened.

"I was on a school field trip, taking a picture at the top of Waterfall Mountain. I slipped and fell down the back side and right past the territory flags."

His eyes widened. "You fell all the way down the back side of Waterfall Mountain?"

I nodded, remembering the pain I'd felt, how horrible the fall was.

"I was so scared, in so much pain. A man with kind blue eyes wearing a bone necklace gave me a bitter, yet sweet herb that took my pain."

He nodded. "Cholka root."

I steeled myself for his reaction to the next part. "He was sifting through his pack to cover me with a blanket because I was shivering, and a group that I later found out to be the Ithaki...beheaded him and took me."

The guy went totally still. He just breathed in a steady rhythm that reminded me of the ocean. His chest rose and fell slowly for a full minute and I swallowed hard, feeling like I was intruding on his grief.

"He was trying to help me, he was a very kind man—"

He held up a hand to stop me; his chest shuddered a little as he worked to control his breathing.

Finally he spoke: "In my culture, we believe that a warrior's soul cannot be free until a witness to their death tells the story of how they passed. Then we tell the story around the full moon once a year forever. The worst thing you can do in my culture is die alone with no story."

Oh God. Had I known that, I would have found them and told them sooner.

"Thank you for doing me the honor of sharing his death story so that his soul can now be free. I will not forget that kindness." He placed a fist to his chest and bowed his head.

I did the same, not wanting to offend him.

"Who...was he?" I asked. The man clearly was important to him. His father? Maybe grandfather?

He sighed. "He was our alpha. The *last* alpha we had. Now our magic will slowly fade with him, as he had no living children."

My eyes widened so big then, I felt like my eyeballs would roll out of my head and onto this wooden bed.

Alpha. Wasn't Run the alpha? Hadn't my mother said he was taking over for his father? Was that man... my grandfather?

My head spun as I tried to figure it all out.

"Shit. I'm so sorry." I didn't know what to say; the revelation was rocking me.

He frowned at me. "I don't understand city girl cuss words. Shit means poop, fuck means sex. Who wants to say poop and sex when they are mad? Why not shout *snakebite* or *murder*?"

I burst out laughing but he looked offended, so I quickly reined it in and tried to turn it into a cough. "No, that's a solid point. I'm definitely going to scream *snakebite* the next time I want to cuss."

He nodded, looking pleased with himself.

"So, you looked like him...the eyes. Were you related?"

He shook his head. "No, all Paladin look similar. Blue eyes, almond shape," he said, and I suddenly felt like an idiot.

What a fucking racist thing to ask him. I wanted to face-palm myself, but I'd never met a Paladin before Waterfall Mountain and I didn't know anything about their kind. It was an innocent question and he seemed to understand that. Probably internally cringing at the stupid city girl.

I gave a nervous laugh.

He stared at me with scrutiny then and I looked away quickly, afraid he might be seeing that *we* had similar eyes, the color and shape. Truth was that striking blue color he had, just on the verge of teal, it stared at me in the mirror every day...the way the corners of my eyes tipped up the slightest bit—it seemed to be a Paladin thing.

"So you're not going to kill me?" I gestured to the gun, changing the subject.

He seemed to forget it was in his hand and set it down on the floor beside me. "Not today." I waited for him to wink to show me he was kidding, but he didn't. This dude was *very* serious.

"Well, on that note, I think I'll try to get some rest," I said, feeling the grogginess pull at my limbs and just being grateful this dude wasn't going to kill me.

He nodded, still watching me funnily. "Where are you going? If you're banished, shouldn't you be kicked out of Magic City?"

Crap. This dude was smarter than I gave him credit for. "It's a long story, but yeah. I'm headed to Delphi

Academy in Spokane, Washington, where I grew up with my parents."

Not exactly a full lie.

He frowned. "You grew up in the human world yet you were taking a class in Werewolf City and fell down Waterfall Mountain?"

Fuck. He looked like he might want to kill me again.

"I got un-banished for a few months, now I'm banished again." I peeled the leather back to show my metal shackles and the angry red skin there.

He frowned, eyes suddenly hardening. "They hurt you? Those poisonous city wolves!"

My eyes widened. "No. This was from vampires. Well, this is my second set. The first one the wolves put on."

He looked confused. "You're complicated," he stated.

I shrugged. "Ain't that the truth."

He reached into his waist pouch and came away with two fingers slicked wet with blue paint. Reaching out, he wiped them across my cheeks and then down the bridge of my nose. "There. Now you might pass for a Paladin trader if you tie up and cover that hair."

This was a very kind thing to do. Maybe paying me back for telling him the alpha's death story. I didn't know, but I suddenly felt emotional.

"Thank you. Where are you headed?"

It's probably like 3 a.m. and I'm tired, but sure, let's do small talk.

He nodded to the left, the way I came. "To Vampire City. They have a job for me."

Chills broke out onto my arms. "Job? You...work with the vampires?"

He looked down his nose at me. "I work with anyone who pays. We in the Wild Lands don't have the luxury to choose alliances."

I shut my mouth, only nodding. I clearly knew nothing about his struggles.

He stood, seemingly done with me. "Goodbye, Mara."

"It's...Demi actually," I told him. "I lied because I was scared you would kill me."

I didn't want to start off my only friendship with a Paladin on lies. His face didn't change when I'd given my real name and I was pretty sure that like the trolls, the Paladin didn't do TV or have phones.

He nodded. "Goodbye, Demi. I hope you make it home." Turning, he crept to the edge of the platform and I suddenly didn't want to be alone in the middle of the night anymore. It was nice to have a friend, or acquaintance, or whatever we were.

"What's your name?" I asked, as he peered over the edge of the platform, the muscles in his back straining under his tight dark skin.

"Arrow." He tipped his head to me, and I tipped mine back, and then he jumped, disappearing into the night like a bird, causing me to scramble to the edge of the platform and peer over the side looking for him.

Show-off.

I had no idea if it was 1 a.m. or 4 a.m., but I felt so tired, it had to be closer to one. With a sigh, I lay back down, trying to fall asleep, but I kept replaying what he'd said in my mind.

He was our alpha. The last alpha we had. Now our magic will slowly fade with him as he had no living children.

Alpha.

Alpha.

Finally, sleep took me, and I welcomed the relief from my own thoughts.

———·—·———

The next morning, I was stiff from sleeping on the hard tree platform but grateful to be alive. There were small tracks from some kind of creature all over the ground and I even spied a dead rat that looked like it had been half eaten. I was worried about Ginny, but she seemed fine as she ate her oats or whatever out of her bag. Whatever pest roamed the ground at night, it didn't like donkey. After peeing at the base of a tree, and brushing my teeth, I was good to go.

This day felt longer than the previous one. The sun was hotter, Ginny felt slower, and I was bored out of my damn mind. Bored, but also on guard for any foe, so super heightened and mentally alert. It was not a good way to feel, and I imagined it would just get worse as I went through the Dark Fey Territory. And when I got there, I wouldn't have Ginny, so I would have to make my way on foot.

This was a nightmare.

How had things taken a turn for the worse so quickly? One second I was making love to Sawyer and we were imprinting, and the next I was like some fugitive on the run from vampires who wanted to drink and bottle my "essence."

What the fuck?

Not to mention the things that Arrow told me last night. That man, the one who saved me...he was the alpha, which could only mean he was my grandfather, right? I was so confused. But either way I wanted to know more about the Paladins. They seemed like a reasonable people. I mean, sure, Arrow almost killed me last night when he thought I was a regular city wolf, but when I told him I was banished, he was cool...

The rift must run really deep between the two clans. Probably what you get for cursing Sawyer's family line.

I was so absorbed in my thoughts, I didn't hear it until it was too late. A whistling sound cut through the air, then hot unyielding pain shot down my spine and an arrow lodged into my injured shoulder. A wild scream ripped from my throat as I lurched forward, lying flat on Ginny's back. "Go!" I yelled and kicked her hard in the ribs with my feet.

She started to run as I fiddled behind me with my good arm and reached for the shotgun. When I felt my fingers grasp around the cool metal, I yanked it from my pack and sat up, spinning around at the same time.

I'd preloaded it this morning, and thank God for that because when I turned, I locked eyes with a giant troll. He was flying through the air, about to jump on my back. Without thinking, I pressed the butt of the shotgun to my good shoulder and pulled the two hammers back before squeezing the trigger with zero hesitation.

Holy crap.

A deafening blast exploded in my eardrums as the base of the shotgun kicked against my shoulder, but I held it firmly in place. A shrill whine rang in my ears, and everything went muffled. At the same time, the two shotgun shells ripped into the chest of the giant male troll and his body flew backward in a heap of blood and flesh.

There were two other trolls running behind their fallen friend, and instead of pressing on to attack me, they stopped to examine his body as Ginny ran like a bat out of hell. I pinched her belly with my thighs, trying to hang on while simultaneously searching for more shotgun shells as blood dripped from my shoulder wound and down my back.

That was a problem for future Demi. I needed to reload in case these asshats tried to come for me like their friend.

The trolls pointed to me and said something, but the

ringing in my ears was so loud, I had no idea what it was. They looked like bandits or something; they wore dirty crude clothing and had traveling packs on their back. Dirt and grease marred their ugly faces with yellowing tusks poking out of their leathery cheeks.

With shaking fingers, I managed to use my elbow to pop open the shotgun and load two new shells. The metal was hot, and I singed my finger before snapping it closed. My poor shoulder was bleeding and hurt like all hell, but I kept my focus. These guys would either fall back or seek revenge.

I waited as Ginny ran into the woods and the men started to heave their friend backward, taking his body with them while they retreated.

Thank God.

I sighed in relief, relaxing only a fraction but still alert. Keeping the gun propped on my lap, I patted Ginny. "You can slow down, girl."

She lessened to a brisk trot and I looked down at my shoulder.

Murderous snakebite! It was bad. Really bad.

The arrow's metal tip had completely protruded through my shoulder, right near my armpit. I peeked behind my back and saw it poking through the other side.

A whimper left my throat as I reached up to probe the wound with gentle fingertips, and pain seared my skin there. Okay, I was leaving it in until I could stop somewhere and figure this out.

'*Sawyer, help,*' I sobbed, and then cried out when the cuffs lit up, stopping my magic.

There was no reply. I was all alone and that was a depressing realization.

Ginny probably saved my life. She trotted double-time, taking me through the forest and finally to a creek where we could take a rest. My legs were so stiff and wobbly I collapsed when I slid off of her. I caught my wavy reflection in the surface of the water.

Holy hell.

I looked like a beaten yet badass warrior. I'd forgotten the blue paint Arrow had placed on my cheeks and the bridge of my nose. The bruise around my eye was an angry purple at the center, fading out to a sickly yellowish green at the edges. The wooden shaft of the arrow jutting out of my shoulder really sealed the deal. If I had my camera, I might even take a picture for shitty memory's sake. I erupted into a fit of laughter, pretty sure I was losing my mind, and then I reached up and grasped the feathered end of the arrow sticking out of my shoulder.

I needed to deal with this. No knight in shining armor was coming to save me. Marmal was far away and I'd run out of luck. This was all me. I had to suck it up and get through this no matter how scary or painful it was.

Reaching down to bite the leather shoulder strap from my arm sling, I braced myself for pain, then I snapped the end of the arrow off.

Murder snake shifter hell! I could no longer cuss

without thinking of Arrow. That dark and mysterious Paladin had me wanting to visit my biological father's people and know more about them.

I groaned as the sharp pain flared to life in my arm and then throbbed down to my elbow and back. Black spots danced in my vision as I fought to stay conscious, and my forehead broke out in sweat.

"Help me," I whimpered, unsure who I was calling out to. God? Sawyer? Ginny? My wolf?

I needed to get these damn cuffs off, but first I had to deal with this arrow. I was afraid if I left it in, it would get infected, but if I pulled it out, I might bleed to death if it had hit an artery.

My breath shook as I looked at sweet Ginny. She was plopped down and drinking from the stream downriver. "What do I do, girl?" I asked her, wondering how I'd survived this long without talking to her. I'd never gone twenty-four hours without a TV or phone or social media. I felt like I was losing my mind.

She looked up at me and then went back to drinking her water. With a shaky hand I filled the canteen in the river and decided that it was impossible to have a main artery in your armpit, right? Your neck yes, your thigh sure—that's where they inserted heart catheters, right? But I'd never heard of a main artery in the armpit. If my smart, premed boyfriend—er ex-boyfriend or whatever he was—were here he could probably tell me, but he wasn't, so...

Digging through the bag Marmal had packed me, I looked to see if she'd left me any more of that salve or anything useful for this moment. Sifting through the brown paper food packages, my eyes fell upon a small leather pouch tied with twine. There was a note hanging off of it.

Just in case you shoot yourself in the foot or get injured.—Love Marmal

Yes! *Please be four Vicodin and a suture kit with a YouTube video explaining how to do stitches on yourself.* Unwrapping the package with one hand took time, but I was able to get it open, and when I saw the contents, I frowned.

Figures.

Instead of Vicodin, there was a chunk of that root that my alleged grandpappy Paladin gave me. What did Arrow call it? Chucka root or something? The other item confused me. It looked like a lighter from the eighteenth century, and a small, four-inch, thin steel rod lay next to it. What was I supposed to do with this and where was the suture kit? I tore a chunk of the root off with my teeth and winced at the initial bitterness before sighing at the sweetness that splashed over my tongue. The root's outside shell was creamy white like ginger, but the inside was bright yellow like turmeric. And its shape was very bulbous. I tried to make mental note of it in case I needed to forage for more. I hoped to be in the safety of Sawyer's arms in a few days, but I had no idea how long it could take if I got into trouble. A week? Longer? Oh God, the thought made depression settle over me like a heavy cloud.

As the root settled into me, making everything feel light, and the pain ebbed a little so that I could focus, I realized what the lighter and steel rod were for.

Oh snakebite. This was gonna hurt.

CHAPTER FOUR

I TOTALLY GOT THIS," I TOLD GINNY, WHO LOOKED AT me from the base of the tree where she was napping. We'd made good time with all the running, but I'd need to get back on her to get across the remainder of Troll Village by nightfall.

I held the lighter in one hand, flame dancing in the afternoon light, while I grasped the steel rod with my nearly useless injured hand, letting the end heat up. I had wrapped a bit of leather around the end so that I didn't burn myself, and now I was just growing the giant set of balls it would take to rip out the arrow and shove the hot steel rod into my wound, giving myself a millionth-degree burn. I think that one was way off the burn chart and into cauterization land. At least I hoped so. There was a small possibility Marmal left me this lighter for a fire and the steel rod just fell in here, but I was too far now to back out.

"I got this. I got this," I chanted. The root was good but not Vicodin good; it was like Tylenol good.

Nervousness danced across my belly as I realized it was now or never. The steel rod was hot and I was wasting lighter fuel.

"I'm a fucking badass bitch who can totally handle this!" I declared to the woods as I felt bile rise up in my stomach.

"One. Two." I clicked off the lighter before I could puss out and dropped it on the forest floor. With my hand free, I reached up and yanked the arrow out of my shoulder from behind, hating the sickening way that it moved inside of my body. It didn't hurt as bad as I thought it might, but the spurt of blood that shot from the wound scared the shit out of me.

Note to self: I guess you do have arteries in your armpit.

Fuck. Fuck. Fuck.

My survival instinct took over then and I just reacted. Dropping the broken, bloody arrowhead to the ground, I grabbed the red-hot steel rod and shoved it into the bleeding hole, crying out in pain as it hissed. The scent of burning flesh hit my nose. Agony like I'd never experienced seeped through my body, but I kept going. I pushed the rod all the way into the hole until it nearly disappeared, and then yanked it back out as the bile in my stomach surged forward.

Pain, *unbelievable* pain, rocked my body as it all

became too much and I turned my head over to the side and vomited.

Ginny made a whining sound and I fell forward, into the cold creek water. The side of my face hit the water and I just let the water run over my face and into my mouth, spitting it out every few seconds. Rolling onto my back, I lay half in and half out of the cold creek as it turned red with my blood. I wondered if I would die like this. Was that blood from my clothes or the wound?

I didn't care.

Everything hurt too much. I just didn't care.

Reaching out with my good arm, I patted the creek edge until my fingers wrapped around the cholka root. Then I put the entire thing in my mouth and started to chew.

Could you overdose on this stuff? Maybe. But I had run out of fucks to give. Not wanting to pass out in the trickling creek, no matter how shallow it was, I rolled onto my side and then forward until I was sort of sitting up.

My chest heaved as dizziness washed over me from the sudden movement, and I knew it was time to do an injury assessment. Using my good fingers, I gently probed the wound and found that it wasn't bleeding. The hole sort of looked closed, but I didn't want to mess with it in case it broke open. It was puckered like a star and angry red. Reaching behind me, I ran my fingers over that hole and they came back slick with a small bit of blood.

Okay...still bleeding back there...but just a little.

I looked around; all I could see for miles were trees, no farms or anyone I could ask for help. Besides, they weren't Marmal, they would surely want the two-million reward and turn me in to the vampires. Instead, I just grabbed a piece of cloth from the sack she'd made me and wadded it into a ball, shoving it into the weeping hole at my back.

A sob escaped me at the throbbing pain that caused, and my hands shook.

I was alive. For now, but I needed to get to the Light Fey City, where I could ask for Prime Minister Locke's help and call Sawyer. Stat.

Grabbing the lighter, bloody steel rod, and arrow tip for memory's sake, I packed them all up and stood slowly. Dizziness washed over me. Ginny stood as well, rushing to my side as I leaned on her. "I gotta get to the border before darkness." I held her and heaved onto her back with what little strength I had left.

She started to walk and the full weight of the Tylenol root crashed into me as I drifted in and out of sleep. Every time Ginny went over a large rock or something, it would shift me and my eyelids would flutter open. Then the soothing back-and-forth motion would start up again and my eyes would close. We did this for several hours until Ginny came to a dead stop and chuffed. My eyelids sprang open as Ginny whined and started to back up. Night was falling. In fact...night was here.

There was barely a sliver of light left through the trees. The woods were washed in a creepy orangish-blue glow, and my gaze fell upon the orange perimeter flags that demarcated the Dark Fey Territory.

I slid off Ginny and pet her behind the ears. "You did good. Good girl." Sticking my hand into her sack of pellet food, I came up with some and she nibbled it from my palm. "Wanna come with me all the way through the fey lands? I'm sure Marmal wouldn't mind so long as I had you returned?" I grabbed the strap nearest her shoulder and began to yank, trying to pull her closer to the border flags, but she reared back and chuffed again.

Dammit.

I looked into the darkening forest; it was different than the troll forest—somehow darker, as if light didn't even go there. The trees didn't move and there was an eeriness in the air.

I'd sort of made friends with Arrow. Maybe I could just cut straight down and across the Wild Lands. Take my chances with the Ithaki. Hope I ran into some Paladin and name-drop Arrow. But they hated city wolves. I doubted they'd let me cross if it meant I was going back there.

I pulled out and consulted the map Marmal had given me. Where I was, it would be twice as long to reach Werewolf City by crossing the entirety of the Wild Lands, and the Ithaki were probably hell-bent on revenge for Butcher's death. No. I just had to push through and do this.

I turned Ginny around, pulled my pack and shotgun off her back, and then gave her one final hug. "You probably saved my life today. Thank you."

Yes. I talked to a donkey because shit had gotten desperate.

With a light smack of her rump, she trotted back into the deep forest of the Troll Village, while I spun on my heel and headed for the Dark Fey Territory. I kept the shotgun in my good hand and only the strap of my pack over my left shoulder, careful not to put any stress on my bad right shoulder.

I could do this. This was fine. I had a shotgun and shotguns killed things. I'm pretty sure I killed that troll today, although I would process that when I was back at Sterling Hill in my dorm with my new therapist that I was totally getting. I peered up at the treetops and noticed there were no more tree house lofts this close to the border. People were smart enough to not sleep near the dark fey. I needed to find a safe space to make camp but not sleep. No way was I even blinking for a long time in this territory. I'd stayed up for all-nighters before with Raven and I could totally do it again.

No matter I'd just gotten shot. I'd be fine.

I'm a badass bitch who doesn't need sleep or stitches.

These pep talks really worked. I felt better already.

With a deep breath, I stepped over the orange flag line and flinched as Sawyer screamed in my head.

'Demi, fucking answer me!'

Relief spread through me as his voice filled me up. I risked the pain I knew was coming to answer him back. *'Just crossed into Dark Fey Territory. Can't talk, it hurts. Got shot with an arrow but I'm okay...I love you.'* The electric shocks seemed to be getting stronger, or maybe that was just my perception, but damn, if we could get these off now, that would be great.

'Demi! Oh, thank fuck. I love you too, I'm restless without you here.' His voice was raspy like he'd been screaming for hours, even if just mentally. He sounded completely worn-out. *'The stupid troll leader is paranoid that the witches read their thoughts, so they put a magical shield over any mind-to-mind connections across their entire territory.'*

A single tear slid down my cheek to hear that it wasn't something I did to mess up our bond, or that he wasn't off on some love ride with Meredith.

'Demi, listen carefully. You have to be very cautious in the dark fey lands. Any amount of your blood that's exposed will lead them right to you.'

Well, wasn't that fucking great. I was covered in blood.

'Don't respond. I'm going to assume if you got shot that you are bleeding.'

That was affirmative.

'I haven't slept since you left,' he rambled on. *'I'm at the border of the Witch Lands with Belladonna Mongrave, the high priestess. She says that if you can steal a fey blade and cut off the cuffs while saying a*

special incantation, it will remove the magic of the cuffs and you can get your powers back and fight.'

Relief rushed through me, but then slowly turned into terror. Steal a fey blade? How the hell would I do that? And how would me speaking the incantation do anything? I wasn't a witch.

'Demi, listen, I had to tell her what you are. That you're half Paladin. Because I know Paladins have witch magic. She said so long as the magic is strong enough in you, it should work.'

I'd never even tried a spell with Raven, it all freaked me out to be honest. I wanted to stick with being a shifter and not dabble in that stuff. But to be free of these chains, I could do it this one time.

'Now the fey blade. It won't look like a knife they cut meat with, it would have a decorative handle or be an ornate type with engravings. Every fey has a fey blade they are given at birth from their fathers.'

Damn, he knew a lot. I nodded as if he could see me. Okay, steal a fey blade from a violent dark fey that turned so evil their own people made them separate and split their lands...no biggie.

My gaze scanned the darkness and found a glow off in the distance that indicated it might be a fire. Maybe I should wait until morning...

'It must be dark there by now, do you see any cabins or tents or anything that shows someone is living inside? Best to do this at night while you have the element of surprise.'

Damn. He really had thought this out.

'*Once you cut them off...*' He paused as if he'd rehearsed this. '*Your scent will become stronger and they'll hunt you.*'

Well, wasn't that the fucking bedtime story I needed.

'*But I've weighed the odds and calculations a hundred times, and you're safer using your powers and having your wolf than if you are trying to hide with the cuffs on, especially if you're bleeding. There's just no way you will make it to the Witch Lands without getting those cuffs off.*'

I stopped walking. Witch Lands? Last time we spoke he said I only had to get to Light Fey City. Maybe that's what he meant. He was just with the witches now and he would meet me in Light Fey City with Prime Minister Locke.

He didn't speak, and his mention of meeting me in the Witch Lands started to bug me.

'*Witch Lands?*' I whispered mentally, hoping that without speaking too loudly, I wouldn't get zapped. No such luck.

He was silent a long time. So much so that I was debating enduring the pain of asking again.

'*We're at war, and the light fey have joined the other side. It's just us and the witches now.*'

I stopped dead in my tracks, hoping I hadn't heard him right.

War? I'd been gone a few days and he'd started a war?

My mother said that if one side ever joined the other, making it four on two, the smaller side would be decimated. I started walking toward the campfire again, if only to keep moving and not freak out too much.

'No. Why? Me?' I hissed as the cuffs burned into my freshly healing skin, but I didn't care. I had to know.

Silence again. I was closer to the fire now. I could see two hulking shapes hunched over the fire and talking softly, so I froze and awaited Sawyer's reply.

'*When I went to Vampire City to retrieve you, Locke stopped me and said I had no legal ground to be there. He put an ankle monitor on me and said that I needed to remain in Wolf City until the murder investigation was over.*'

An ankle monitor. Holy shit.

'*So I killed him.*'

Oh. My. God.

'*Sawyer! You didn't!*' I hissed at the pain from the cuffs.

I could feel his anger threading through our imprint, raw and unbridled. '*Oh yes, I did. We found out he's been in league with the vampires since the night he met you. They both want you and are willing to work together to get you. He tried to keep me from rescuing you, so I took him out of the equation. No one's going to get in the way of my bringing you home safely, Demi. No one.*'

My boyfriend went on revenge murder sprees more than I liked to admit, but it was kind of sweet.

'Demi...' His voice broke. 'I've tried everything I can think of. Our helicopter was shot down... This fucking ankle bracelet electrocutes me if I try to leave Werewolf City. We're working on getting it off, and I sent Sage and Walsh to try and find you, knowing you would be along the dark fey border but...' His voice broke and my heart pinched. I just wanted him to hold me. I just wanted to erase the past few days and start over. Poor Sage and Walsh were tied up in this now, and everyone was at war. This wasn't right.

He sighed. 'But all of this is a long shot... I think you're going to have to make it to me on your own.'

My heart thundered in my chest to hear that I might be alone all the way to the Witch Lands. That was *two* more territories over. I'll be honest, I'd been hoping for a helicopter rescue, but hearing that one got shot down... that option was gone.

'Can you do that? Can you be strong and make it back to me?' There was an ache in his voice that I felt in my bones. 'Because I'm not sure I can live in a world without you.' He mentally sobbed. 'And I definitely can't live with myself and how I treated you the last time we saw each other.'

Silent tears slid down my face and I nodded.

'Don't answer,' he added. 'These things hurt like hell if it's anything like my ankle bracelet. When you *get home, I'm banishing them forever. And I'm bringing your parents home and I'm never letting you out of my sight again.'*

A sob escaped my throat, but I swallowed the noise for fear of alerting the two giant figures sitting around the campfire. How had everything gone to shit so fast? It was so nice to hear him back to his raging, jealous, murderous self.

'I prayed,' he went on, probably finally elated he could speak to me again. And to be honest, I needed the human contact and needed to hear everything he was thinking. It was nice to just listen for once. *'I'm not even religious and I prayed you would return to me unharmed,'* he said.

I smiled, imagining Sawyer with clasped hands sending up a prayer for me. He really was a catch, but I did wonder one thing...

'Meredith...?' My arms were going to fall off at this point. I'd never been consistently electrocuted so much in my entire life, but I had to know. I had to know if that bitch just got a slap on the wrist for her stunt.

His anger bled through our bond, *'She's been banished from Wolf City forever at my request. She'll be enrolled in Delphi University tomorrow.'*

Shock ripped through me. He...*banished* her for that? I didn't know what to say. Was she cuffed? Was she all alone? I kind of suddenly felt bad for her even though she totally tried to ruin my relationship.

'I should have believed you, Demi, I should have known. I feel you in my soul. I know what you are capable of and what you aren't. I should have known better even through a stupid spell.'

You can't just see through spells though, that's not how they work. We just sat there in silence for another few minutes, breathing and just being. I wasn't going to hold it against him. He had been under some magical love spell, and it did look like I'd kissed another guy. Well, I *had* kissed another guy, but that whole situation was fucked, and if I ever saw that douchebag again, it was a kick right to the nuts.

I was ready to move on from this and get my life back, my boyfriend back. If we broke up over this, Meredith won.

I was also ready to get these damn cuffs off. Eyeing the two figures by the fire, I worked slowly to pull off my pack, and set it at the base of the tree I was leaning against, making sure to be quiet. The two figures ahead were talking softly, and muffled, so that I couldn't understand them while cooking something on the low fire.

What did Sawyer say? Every fey had a fey blade? I wondered if I just walked up and asked to borrow it for two seconds if they would let me... Yeah right. These were *dark* fey, fey that did such evil shit their eyes turned black from the magic and they separated from their light fey kin to run their own sick territory. The horror stories that they told at Delphi about this place gave me the creeps. They'd put the Ithaki to shame if they were true. My gut feeling said that if I wanted to live through this night, I'd have to wait until they fell asleep. The shotgun was nice, but it wasn't going to work well on two people. Two *dark fey* of all people. They'd have me frozen in place with magic by the time I could reload.

There were very few dark fey at Delphi; they didn't usually banish their kind that broke the rules; they just killed them.

I slowly slid to the base of the tree and clutched the shotgun on my lap. I just wanted my wolf. If I had full use of my powers, I wouldn't need to be so afraid. I'd still be scared shitless about sleeping the night here, but not this overwhelming helpless feeling I had now.

I spent the next hour or so tapping a soundless rhythm on my thighs. I wasn't prepared for the cold wind that blew through the trees at night and had to keep my teeth clenched in an effort to keep them from chattering. This was a waiting game and I had to win in order to get the blade. I was initially afraid of falling asleep while waiting, but it was so damn cold there was no way that was happening. Also, the Tylenol root had worn off and the pain of my injury was coming on strong.

Once I felt enough time had passed, I stood and slowly stretched my legs. They were stiff, but nothing like the throbbing pain in my shoulder. I needed to find more of that root, and I prayed I could get these cuffs off and heal before any permanent damage or infection.

I stared at the small dying embers of the fire and was glad to see the two huge figures seemed to be lying down, hopefully asleep. They didn't have a dog or anything like that with them, which was good, because I heard the fey had familiars of all kinds, and I couldn't deal with killing anything more than I had to right now. The two dark fey I knew of from Delphi had their familiars killed before they were banished.

I shivered.

Leaving my pack at the base of the tree, I slowly cocked the hammers back on the shotgun. I wasn't going to ask questions. If either one of those giant bundles of sleeping cloth moved, I was shooting.

Fey blade. Fey blade.

Focus. Just get the blade and get out, I told myself.

As I crept closer, I relished the warmth of the dying fire. Maybe I could sit here for a minute and warm up. My eyes immediately went to the large packs that lay just a few feet from the sleeping figures. There were two places I would keep a special dagger. In my pack or on my body.

I was going to check the pack first before groping a sleeping man.

I tried to make as little noise as possible, but still a few leaves crinkled under my feet and I froze each time, staring at the two sleeping men. They wore animal skins, pulled over their heads so I couldn't see their faces.

I inhaled. *Deer.* Deer furs, freshly skinned. I could

still smell the blood on them, and it made me sick. It also masked their smell, which was smart.

Get the blade and get out. My eyes roamed the packs and excitement bubbled up inside of me at the sight of a glint of steel.

Tiptoeing over to the pack, with the two sleeping figures and the warm fire at my back, I crouched down ever so quietly and grabbed for the glint of steel that I'd seen. As I was pulling it out, I heard movement at my back. Not a small rolling over while asleep movement. Someone had awoken and was launching across the rocky ground to grab me. As the sound of scrambling feet filled my ears, I brought the shotgun up and spun around.

My finger was on the trigger, about to pull, when a shock of red hair tumbled out of the hood of deer fur.

It made me hesitate because it reminded me of Sage.

The deer-fur-covered person froze, yanking her hood back, and a strangled cry flew from her lips. "Demi?"

Everything in me shut down then. I'd been running for two days purely on adrenaline, and upon seeing Sage, upon knowing I was no longer in this alone, I just ran out of steam, ran out of strength. Lowering the shotgun, I fell to my knees, sobbing. Sage crumpled to the ground beside me and wrapped her arms around me gently, seemingly unsure how injured I was. She started to rock back and forth slowly like you would if you were holding a child.

I'm not alone. That's all I could think. *I'm not alone anymore.*

"We're here now. It's okay. We got you," she whispered.

Movement passed behind her and she looked up. "She's shaking with cold. Get the extra fur," Sage barked to the second figure, who I assumed was Walsh. I couldn't see through the blurry landscape of my tears.

Two seconds later, a warm fur was thrown over me, bringing that nasty freshly killed smell with it.

"It hides our wolf smell from the fey. They hunt our kind for use in spells," she told me.

Great. Hunted no matter what I was. Just freaking great.

I didn't stop crying. I couldn't. I felt so fragile and broken and embarrassed. But neither of them said anything. She just held me while Walsh kept the fur draped around my shoulders and no one said anything about my nervous breakdown.

It was a few moments before anyone spoke. "I smell your blood, Demi," Walsh's deep voice called behind me. "Are you injured?"

I sniffled, pulling back from Sage and wiping gently at my eyes, wincing when I hit the injured socket the queen had punched. I just nodded, unable to be strong anymore knowing I had others to lean on. Sage looked beat up as well, bruises on her cheeks; her hair was matted in parts with mud, and her nails had dried blood under them. She probably had a story to share about getting here as well.

Walsh crouched in front of me, strong and silent Walsh, here for me. Sawyer's best friend. I felt so emotional I reached out and pulled him in for a hug. His arms were limp at first, as if I'd shocked him. Then he gave me two quick pats on the back and pulled away, clearing his throat.

"Where are you bleeding? I have a med-kit," he asked again.

I nodded and pulled the fur back to show him my shoulder.

He hissed. "We need to get these cuffs off so your werewolf healing can kick in."

Sage scurried to her pack and produced a piece of paper. "Sawyer said if we found you to give you this. It's the incantation to remove the cuffs. We just need to find a fey blade."

I looked down at the steel I'd dropped when going through their packs to find it was a regular old hunting knife.

I nodded to her, taking the incantation and folding it up before shoving it in my pocket. "I can't...believe you're here."

Sage grinned. "It's that or I go to Magic City Jail for murdering Meredith. Sawyer thought sending me on a recon mission was a better idea."

More tears spilled from my eyes. She was a good friend.

"I would never cheat on Sawyer. Ever," I told her.

She nodded, eyes going watery. "I'm sorry I didn't say anything right away. I was…so shocked. I mean, it all happened so fast, and by the time I started to question things you were gone. I chased after you and Eugene but lost your trail."

I nodded and squeezed her hand. "It's okay. We were all tricked."

She looked guilty as hell, and I wished I could take that feeling from her. It wasn't her fault.

"When I finally got to talk to Sawyer, he was *so sure* Meredith was the one…his love. He kept talking about the stupid necklace. I knew everything was wrong then, that magic was at play."

I nodded. I hoped it was currently at the bottom of a lake somewhere or bashed into a billion pieces.

I smiled. "He said you punched him in the face?"

A slow grin pulled at her lips. "'No, don't touch the necklace, it's my special present.'" Sage mocked Sawyer's deep voice and clutched at her neck as if reenacting the scene. "Homeboy was brainwashed. I knew then I had to get that thing off of him."

Walsh chuckled and pointed to my eye. "You and Sawyer have matching shiners."

Okay, I totally forgave Sawyer, because it wasn't his fault, but somewhere deep inside of me I felt a little spark of joy at Sage punching him.

Walsh pressed lightly on my shoulder and I hissed.

"Your back is still bleeding. I need to suture it." Walsh probed my wound further and I whimpered.

Sage looked at me sadly. "Can't we wait until we find a blade to cut off her cuffs?"

Walsh shook his head. "That could take us all night, and she's lost a lot of blood. Her whole back is crusted with it. She needs sutures *now.*"

Oops...

At that comment, dizziness washed over me. How much blood had I lost? How long until we could find a blade? Was this going to hurt? What could possibly hurt more than sticking a hot poker into the front of my shoulder?

"Were you?" He paused. "Shot or...?"

I nodded. "With an arrow, and then I burned it with a hot poker to stop the bleeding."

Both of their eyes widened.

"Damn." Walsh appraised me with pride.

"Just do it quickly please," I said through gritted teeth.

Walsh nodded. "Sawyer sent a morphine patch, but I'm afraid with your cuffs on it might hit you too hard, like it would a human, and you won't be alert enough to—"

I shook my head. "Is there Tylenol?"

He reached into a small red canvas med bag and gave me two pills with a bottle of water. I greedily gulped them down.

"Want me to wait twenty minutes until it kicks in?" he asked.

I chuckled. Two Tylenol weren't going to do shit for the feeling of being sewn up while awake. "No. Let's just get it over with."

He appraised me with pride and nodded.

Sage reached out her hands and clasped them with mine, looking up at my face. She smiled dryly. "You almost shot me. Where did you get the gun?"

I chuckled, welcoming the distraction when I felt Walsh's cold hands pinch the skin in my back together. "Met a friend in Troll Village. She gave it to meahh-hhhh—" I screamed as sharp, shooting pain sliced through my shoulder. Sage's hand yanked from mine and clamped it over my mouth as sweat beaded my brow.

"He'll be quick. Just breathe through your nose," Sage cooed with her hand still over my mouth.

Another sharp pain stabbed into my shoulder and I half screamed, half sobbed. I didn't think it would hurt this bad, but I was so wrong. It was like getting a lip ring torn out and then getting it re-pierced the same day. Too many wounds in one already sensitive spot.

"I thought you were a Paladin with that blue paint," Sage commented. "Did your troll friend help you with that too?" she asked as two more short stabs entered my shoulder.

I just nodded, unable to focus on what she was

saying, trying to keep conscious and as quiet as possible. Talking about Arrow right now was not a good idea.

"Done," Walsh said. "I'm going to put some disinfectant on it. Shouldn't burn too bad since I've already closed it."

Oh hell no. The word disinfectant always meant burn like a motherfucker. Sage's hand tightened over my mouth as cold liquid washed over my shoulder and trickled down my back. It felt like someone had poured gasoline on my back and lit it on fire. I had no more strength to scream, so I just huffed and groaned into Sage's hand while squeezing her other in a death grip.

Sawyer suddenly surged into my brain and I whimpered as the pain in my shoulder finally eased. *'I fell asleep by accident. Why does it feel like you are being skinned alive! Talk to me, Demi!'* I lay forward on Sage's lap, breathing in and out softly as she stroked my hair. I felt sick, like I was going to vomit.

"All done. You're okay now."

I couldn't take any more pain, but I also couldn't let Sawyer think I was dying.

'Sage. Walsh. Stitches,' was all I managed as the cuffs lit up and shocked my arms, causing me to whimper again.

'Oh thank God! They found you! Demi, that's amazing. I'm so sorry you're hurting, but Walsh is a trained field medic. He will take good care of you while I can't be there.' There was relief and sadness in his voice. I knew as a premed student he was probably aching to

do the stitches himself, but also that he just wanted to protect me.

"What the fuck was that!" Sage looked at the cuffs on my wrists with wide eyes.

I looked up at her, wondering if she really wanted to know. "Every time…I try to shift or do anything magical, including talking to Sawyer, it electrocutes me."

Her eyes widened and she and Walsh shared a pitying look.

"Well, don't do that anymore. He'll be fine now that he knows you're with us," she assured me.

Walsh scoffed. "He won't be fine until she's in his arms and every last vampire in connection with her kidnapping is burned alive."

I was about to respond when we all heard it. A twig snapped to the left and we all went stock-still, not uttering a single word. The only sound that could be heard was the snapping of Walsh's bones. He tore off his deer furs and shifted while I sat up from Sage's lap and grabbed for my shotgun. Sage sprang into a standing position and pulled a giant katana sword from behind her. I'd never seen her actually protect anyone from harm. I mean, I knew she was studying security at Sterling Hill, but seeing her hold that katana in a crouched stance, I wondered how badass she would be in action.

Three cloaked figures stepped into the moonlight; dark hoods obscured their faces. I stood on wobbly feet and held my gun up, resting it on my good shoulder.

"We're Paladin traders, just passing through. We don't want trouble," I told them as my thumb fidgeted with the hammers on the shotgun, only to find they were already cocked back from when I almost shot Sage.

One of them pulled back their hood and terror ripped through me. It was a woman. A woman with translucent pale skin and a network of...black *glowing* veins. It was hard to describe what I was looking at, but it wasn't a person. It was a creature. She had the stereotypical pointed dark fey ears and black eyes, but everything else about her screamed something else.

"The demon speaks," she said to her friends, and my blood went cold. That's what the Ithaki called me.

My blood, they must smell whatever I am in my blood.

Walsh's wolf peeled his lips back and gave a low growl, while Sage stepped in front of me protectively. The fey opened her mouth to speak, but instead of words, a black blob flew from her lips and opened like a net about to catch a fish.

What the fuck?

It was headed right for Sage, sickly black and... *alive* looking. As it arced through the air I could see it... *moving*. The rope in the netting was *squirming*.

I didn't think. I just reacted. Stepping out from behind Sage, I jumped in front of her just as the net reached me. With a smack it slammed into me and molded around my form like shrink wrap, oozing onto my skin like a glove. A sickly feeling fell over me and I panicked, pulling the trigger of the shotgun. It blew out the tip of the net, which only caused the blackness to clamp down on me harder.

A hiss shattered the night air, and I looked out through the netting that was now over my face to see I'd blown the dark fey's left arm clean off.

Score.

"Put your arms out like a starfish!" Sage barked at me randomly, and I did as she asked, wincing as the net clamped down and tried to force my arms to my side.

Sage pulled her katana and held it low, near my feet. I was confused until she brought it between my ankles and then sliced upward, shredding the net that held my legs.

"Nooo!" the fey shrieked and my gaze flicked to see her holding her bleeding shoulder stump, the place where I'd blown her arm clean off. But that didn't seem to be what bothered her, because her gaze was on Sage cutting the net. She cried out in pain as if Sage hurting the net hurt *her*. The two other fey had been seemingly frozen in shock at my shotgun blast, but they now rushed forward and Walsh leapt from the shadows in wolf form, taking one of them down to the ground.

"Incoming!" I warned Sage of the fey running at us as she hacked away at the black net, trying to free my good hand, the one that held the shotgun.

She spun just in time to confront the black, hooded figure. He pulled a matte black sword, something I could barely see in the dying firelight, and they traded blows back and forth. I scrambled to free my arm and wiggle out of the squirming net, horrified to see that it left black trails of ink on my skin. That smell...was that *blood?* Was this net fucking made of dark fey *blood?*

Bile and panic rose up inside of me as I scrambled to reach into my pocket where I'd shoved a few shotgun shells. This fucking net was clinging to me like a squid, wet and suctioning, but my bigger worry was the one-armed bitch walking over to me with murder in her eyes.

I opened the gun with shaking fingers and shoved two shells inside, snapping it shut just as she reached me.

Pulling the hammers back, I raised my arm, ready to blow her head off.

She looked at me, black blood spurting from her limbless shoulder, and grinned like she was losing her mind. Her teeth were razor sharp, and translucent. She was basically my worst nightmare. Why was she grinning at me? Maybe she wanted to die.

She took one more step and I pulled the trigger.

But nothing happened.

Panic surged inside of me as my gaze flicked to the gun for a millisecond to see the black net had crawled up my hand and was holding the hammers back.

Shit.

When I looked back at her, she was already too close. With a maniacal scream, she slammed into my chest and knocked me backward.

I could only think of one thing as I fell backward and my head cracked the ground: *How is she still alive with one arm and bleeding like that?*

Pain exploded in my skull, but I didn't have time to dwell on it. Bitch was coming at me hard. This was life or death, fight or flight.

My wolf wanted free, she wanted to show this demon what we were capable of. But I would have to do instead. The dark fey barreled at me and I kicked both of my feet right into her stomach as she tried to crawl on top of me. She grunted as my feet rammed into her gut, and then crumpled to the ground as I pushed her backward.

I popped onto my knees, using the shotgun like a baseball bat and swinging, cracking her upside her temple. Then I tore the black netting away from the hammers and brought the barrel to her forehead.

Bye, bitch.

I pulled the trigger and the gun kicked back into my shoulder as the force of the weapon blasted into her face. Bits of her brain exploded onto the ground. My ears whined at the loud bang and I stepped back in case she was going to pull some Terminator shit and regrow a brain or something. When the black netting started to disintegrate and fall to the ground in ashes, I knew she was finally dead.

Looking up to see if Sage and Walsh needed help, I was relieved to see their kills on the ground as well.

Both looked at me, wide-eyed. No way would I have survived all three of those dark fey without Sage and Walsh's help. Thank God I'd run into them.

"Are all dark fey like that?" I asked them both as I tried to get my heart rate back to a normal rhythm.

Sage shook her head. "Those were Munai, the dark fey high priestesses. It takes decades of dark magic studying to become a Munai."

Well, that was horrifying, but also a relief. The Denai were the dark sect of witches, and the Munai were the dark sect of fey. The names were familiar, and I wondered if it was a coincidence. Probably not.

I shivered thinking of the black netting and how it had flown from her mouth and seemed to be alive and connected to her. Gross.

"Get her fey blade and let's move. Anyone within earshot will have heard that shotgun." Walsh was human again and throwing his furs back over him.

Fey blade.

My eyes went to the dead body of the Munai. There at her hip was a small, dark gray metal dagger. It wasn't a shiny silver, it appeared more like titanium; the hilt was heavily decorated and ornate.

Did I really want to use the dagger of a dead, dark fey high priestess? No. Did I have a choice right now?

Also no.

Reaching down, I pulled the dagger from her hip and immediately felt the magical power from it. I could smell it as well, as if I were holding an electrical wire. The buzz of magic thrummed through it as the scent of hot wires reached my nose.

I swallowed hard and pulled out the incantation Sage had given me from Sawyer.

Please work.

Please. *Fucking*. Work.

My wolf surged to the surface in excitement and a jolt of electricity shot out from the cuff, causing me to whimper. She retreated and I felt her shame at causing me harm. I wanted to tell her it was okay, but mental speak would earn me another shock no doubt.

"We gotta move. Get those cuffs off." Walsh doused the fire and hefted my pack as well as his own onto his back.

Without ceremony, I took the tip of the dagger and ran it down the cuff on my right arm like Madam Harcourt had that first day at Sterling Hill. It cut into the hard steel like butter and the cuff fell to the ground.

Relief surged through me at the sight of seeing the broken cuff by the fire. I switched hands, slower this time, as it was not my dominant arm. My poor arms were so red and bloody, I didn't want to injure myself further. When the second cuff fell to the ground, I half sobbed in relief.

Slipping the dagger into the back of my belt, I pulled out the piece of paper from my pocket that Sage had given me. I knew it was going to hurt—I'd nearly passed out when Eugene had held me in place when Madam Harcourt had removed them before—but I just had to push through a little bit more pain.

Without wasting any time, I rattled off the witch-speak: "*Entora dilumin wolven forchesto.*" I sucked in a short breath as searing pain wove through each limb. I clamped my teeth shut with a crack and swayed on my feet. Sage stepped closer to me as I panted, breathing through the sharp stinging agony, black dots dancing at the edges of my vision.

"*Wolven risenoto becara.*" A yelp left my throat, and I knew it was just too much. Too much trauma too close to each other. The black dots became bigger and then everything went black.

CHAPTER FIVE

I CAME TO IN WALSH'S ARMS. HE WAS HOLDING ME like a baby, cradled to his chest with the furs draped around us.

"We need to bathe all of this blood off her!" he snapped to Sage. "She's like a beacon."

My body bounced up and down and I realized he was running.

"I'm awake," I mumbled, flinching with pain each time my body slammed down into his and my shoulder wound pressed into his chest.

He looked down at me with a sharp gaze. "Can you run?"

Run? Maybe…

"I could definitely walk fast…"

"Fuck it," he growled, and pulled me tighter to

him as he pumped his legs faster. I felt weak, tired, and absolutely overjoyed to see my wrists were free of the cuffs.

My wolf.

I peered over to see Sage shooting an arrow from a bow that I hadn't noticed before.

That meant…someone was chasing us.

My wolf surged to the surface and I braced myself for the pain that never came. The spell was gone and I wanted to weep for joy, but there was no time.

Fur broke out onto my arms and Walsh must have felt it against his chest, because he looked down at me. "If your wolf's coming out, tell her to run ahead and find us a cabin or something to wash you up in."

I nodded as a muzzle took shape before my face and then pulled away from my body, going spectral. My wolf form leapt out of Walsh's arms, as he still clung to my human body, and before she hit the ground she was fully formed.

'I'll find a cabin or a creek,' she said and then took off, vampire-fast, into the woods ahead of us.

I felt some strength return now that the cuffs were off and my powers were on full display. I could feel my werewolf healing kick in.

"I think I can run now," I told him.

He looked over at Sage, who was covered in black blood and jogging apace with us. "I think I got the last one."

90

Last one of what? Were more of those creatures chasing us? I shivered.

Walsh skidded to a stop and set me down just as Sawyer's presence surged forward. *'I fell asleep again. Are you okay?'*

'Cuff's off, but still in some shit. Mind text you later,' I told him, and started to jog lightly.

I could almost see him smiling, that chin butt on full display. *'Mind text you later. I love you.'*

I smirked. I'd probably never get used to hearing those words.

"Did another Munai come?" I asked Sage.

She shook her head. "Just a regular dark fey who apparently had a bear as a pet." She lifted her arm so that I could see three deep gashes from wrist to elbow.

Shit.

Who kept a wild bear as a pet? A freaking dark fey, that's who.

My wolf pulled on my thoughts and I attuned my attention to her. She was inside of a hunting cabin. It was cold and looked abandoned, but it had a fireplace and stack of wood.

"We've got a cabin for the night. This way." I veered to the left and followed my wolf's inner sense of direction. She'd jumped through a window to break into the house and had gotten some cuts in her fur. I wondered why she didn't walk through the front door like she'd walked through the glass back on campus to help Sawyer.

'*With you injured, I need to conserve our magic.*' She told me as she read my thoughts.

Whoa.

She had her nose to the ground, sniffing out the place and checking every room. She smelled some type of dried meats in a cupboard and a gamey animal smell under the floorboards. Probably something like a rat. There was a thick layer of dust over everything. It looked like whatever this place was, it was a seasonal cabin, or abandoned.

As Walsh, Sage and I came upon the small A-frame structure then, I switched from my wolf vision to human.

"There." I pointed. It was barely visible in the dark moonlight, surrounded by trees.

"Empty?" Walsh asked.

I nodded. "Yep."

Sage shook her head. "That's seriously so cool that you can do that."

I gave her a weak smile; it was hard to think something you did was cool when you were constantly being hunted for it.

When we reached the door, I tried it, only to find it locked.

Duh.

Peering into the broken window, I spotted my wolf waiting by the fireplace for me. I slipped my hand into the open window and turned the lock, unlocking the door.

Once we got inside, Walsh got right to work on stitching up Sage's arm while I cleaned up the glass with a handmade broom I found in the closet and patched the window with cardboard to keep the heat in. My wolf lay by the fireplace just watching us, seemingly content with being outside of my body right now. It was weird to be apart. I felt slightly uncomfortable without her with me. Like I was hungry, or tired, or half full. It was hard to explain. As if she heard my thoughts, which I'm sure she did since we were the same person, she trotted over to me.

'*We will heal faster together.*' Then she leapt into the air, went transparent, and settled inside my chest.

"That's unreal," Walsh commented, and I turned to see him and Sage watching me with complete and utter fascination.

I gave a nervous laugh. "Should I start a fire?"

Walsh shook his head. "I'll put on the fire and burn everything that has your blood on it. You need to wash up. I lit the pilot light on the water heater in the basement, but I'm not sure if it will work. It's ancient."

I nodded.

He reached into his pack and pulled out some of my clothes. "From Sawyer," he said.

I looked down and smiled, tears filling my eyes. It was my "Feeling Stabby" T-shirt and black cargo pants. Plus a new pair of Converse shoes, sans duct tape heel. There was also a sports bra and clean undies.

He'd thought of everything. I realized now that as much as I was going through hell here, he was in his own hell trying to manage this situation from afar. If the roles were reversed, I would be losing my mind being unable to help him.

Grabbing the fresh clothes, careful not to get blood on them, I slipped into the bathroom and ran the water, praying to every god imaginable that the water heater worked.

It *did*. Warm, fresh water hit my chest and I nearly cried out in joy.

Bless the lord, it did!

There was a bar of handmade soap on the ledge, and although it grossed me out to use it, I knew I had no other options. I just told myself it wasn't previously used by a dark fey. Working the bar between my hands, I scraped off the first few layers with my thumbnail and let it slide down the drain. Then I stepped into the warm water and lathered my entire body, being careful when going over the wounds at the front and back of my shoulder. The water rolled down my back and legs, pooling a pinkish red at the base of the tub.

Walsh was right, I had lost *a lot* of blood with this shoulder wound. I mean, I was shot with a fucking arrow, so I'm not sure what I expected, but...damn. Even the ends of my hair were dyed pink from sitting at the back of my shirt and soaking up blood. It took a long time, and lots of awkward and painful reaching, but I was able to get it all off my back...I hoped. I used the bar soap in my hair, which left it uber dry, and without conditioner I knew I would have a rat's nest, but zero fucks given because this was survival mode. Considering yesterday I'd "showered" in a stream next to a mule, this was a five-star resort.

Sawyer spoke just as I turned off the tap: *'I miss you. I can't believe this situation got so fucked so fast.'*

I sighed, wringing out my hair and using a towel that hung on the wall to pat myself dry.

'I miss you too. We'll be okay. We'll get through this,' I told him.

He was quiet, and I felt his guilt thrumming through our bond. *'Do you ever wish I left you at Delphi? I feel like I...I ruined your life.'*

My heart pinched. *'Never. Not in a million years, Sawyer. If you didn't get me out of there, I never would have been free and I never would have found love. Aren't those like two basic principles of happiness?'*

I could almost feel him grinning. *'So you're saying I did you a favor? Maybe you owe me.'*

I snorted. *'I wouldn't go that far.'*

He was quiet while I dressed, and I wondered what else was bothering him. *'What's going on with you? Everything okay near the Witch Lands?'*

He sighed, and there was a pause where I could feel him sifting through what to tell me. *'Sawyer, what's going on?'*

'I've been escorted back to Sterling Hill, where I'm on house arrest. I can't leave the school grounds until my trial for Vicon Drake's murder.'

Holy fuck. *'Sawyer, it's all good, I blew up the evidence room when I was with the vampires.'*

I briefly gave him a rundown of the room with the briefcase and fur in it and how I'd made it all go poof.

'You did that for me?' he asked finally. *'Even after what happened with Meredith?'*

'Of course!' I admonished. *'True mates, remember?'*

'That was...very sweet, Demi, but they'd already gotten the results and sent them to the Magic City Crime Division. Then when I showed up and tried to bring you home, they pulled some fur off my wolf to confirm...'

No.

No, no, no.

'What are you saying?' I couldn't think straight, I couldn't put two and two together.

His sorrow pushed through our bond. *'I'm saying that I'm on trial for assassinating the prince of Vampire City. If found guilty, I'll spend the next twenty years in Magic City Jail.'*

I shook my head back and forth vigorously. *'No. Vicon raped me. We filed a complaint. Have your useless lawyer pull that file. He should be in jail. Not you. And like you said, the sentence in Vampire City for brutal rape is death.'*

'The rape would have to be proven in court,' he told me.

I nodded. 'I'll testify, so can Raven and my mother and father. The local human hospital in Spokane did a rape kit. I will not let you take the fall for killing that awful animal.'

I could feel the barely contained anger brewing inside of him and I knew it wasn't anger at me. It was anger at Vicon and Queen Drake, and the system. 'Look, I don't want you to worry about this. Just get to the Witch Lands. Your mother and Raven are waiting to greet you. They will bring you to me. Just focus on surviving, Demi. They will do everything in their power to take you from me.'

Survive. Wasn't that my middle name now? I could do this. I could make it back to him. I would make sure he wasn't going anywhere.

I whimpered. 'Why...why do they want me so badly?'

He sighed. 'About a hundred reasons. You're a split shifter and they want your power. They'll use you like a battery, draining you every day to fill themselves up. They also know that if I don't get married, my entire family line dies and our wolves will have no alpha, which will make our race easier to control.'

Well, if that wasn't just awful, I didn't know what was.

'I got this. I'll see you soon. Promise,' I told him, and then stepped out into the living room to find Sage in Walsh's lap, *kissing* him.

Holy mother.

I cleared my throat and she jumped off of him like she'd been stung, wiping at her red lips. "What's up?" she said, her voice cracking. "Shower have hot water? Did you get all the blood off? I'm next. I think I'll head in." She blasted past my grinning face with her crimson cheeks and shut herself in the bathroom.

I looked at Walsh, who looked surprisingly calm as he watched the flames of the fire flickering to the top of the stone. I decided to let this go and get the details later from Sage.

"I talked to Sawyer," I told Walsh. "He's on house arrest now in Werewolf City. Can't leave until his hearing."

Walsh's eyes went stormy. "That's bullshit. That vampire had it coming."

I'd forgotten until this moment that Walsh had been on that "hunting trip" with Sawyer.

"You think it's just about Vicon, or also because he killed the prime minister?"

Walsh shook his head. "He was well within his right to kill Locke. The guy lost his mind and physically tried to hold him back from inspecting the building we thought you were in. We had evidence and he shut the whole thing down. Locke threw the first punch, went feral like a strung-out junkie."

I frowned. That was...wild and weird. It was so obvious that the people running these cities were corrupt as all hell.

"What does Sawyer's dad think of all this? He must be...pissed at me."

Walsh scoffed. "All due respect to my alpha...but he's too soft. Sage's dad would have been a better fit, and Sawyer will be an amazing leader. Curt brushes things under the rug and is always avoiding fights. He's known for being a pushover, so the other leaders push him around."

I winced. That was basically what I'd seen of the alpha as well. "So he doesn't really care?"

Walsh shrugged. "He's deferring to Sawyer on everything. I think he can't wait for his son to take over next year."

Geez, that was not what the largest city of werewolves needed, a weak alpha. I was glad Sawyer was stepping up, but killing the prime minister, declaring war, and then being put on house arrest, wasn't exactly in the plan.

"You should try to get some rest. That shoulder will heal faster with some sleep. I'll keep watch." He tipped his head toward the fire, where he'd laid out a few sleeping bags. A yawn escaped me at the mere mention of sleep, and I nodded.

A few hours wouldn't hurt. "Thanks," I told him, and took a sip of water from my canteen before slipping into the warm sleeping bag. It smelled like Walsh; he must have given me his. I set a mental clock for three hours so I could wake up and take a shift so Walsh could get some sleep.

Suddenly, the weight of the day pressed down on me. Killing the troll after getting shot, then sticking a hot poker in my own arm, then killing the dark fey. It was all too much.

'*Gonna sleep a bit. Walsh keeping watch. Love you.*'

''*Kay, me too.*' Sawyer's reply was instant. '*And I really fucking love hearing you say that you love me.*'

I fell asleep with a grin on my face.

CHAPTER SIX

I AWOKE TO THE SOUND OF A BANGING METAL POT AND
the smell of coffee.

Coffee.

My eyelids snapped open to see Walsh pouring thick
black liquid into three steaming mugs. Then he poured
some powdered cream and sugar packets into all of
them.

"You have coffee!" I sat up and reached my hands
out greedily for a mug.

He chuckled and I could see why Sage found him
handsome. He was good looking in that rugged, I-don't-
talk-and-I-look-like-an-axe-murderer way.

"I like to be prepared," was all he said, and handed
me a mug.

Sage walked out of the bathroom then, wearing tight
yoga pants and a white T-shirt with no bra. Her red hair

was pulled high into a messy topknot and she held a toothbrush in her hand. She was effortlessly beautiful, and I didn't miss how his eyes raked over her body as she spoke.

"Walsh is a prepper. He's probably got a sewing kit in his pack."

Walsh scowled at her. "I do. Because sewing kits are useful in emergencies."

Sage grinned, looking way too beautiful for this hour. "The next time I have an emergency button that needs mending, I'll run right over." She reached out and grabbed her mug from him and took a sip.

He chuckled. "You haven't gone through senior year survival training yet. You'll see. That shit will break you."

Sage looked slightly terrified but brushed it off.

"Senior year survival training?" I asked.

Walsh flicked his gaze to me. "When you become Sawyer's wife, they'll make you take it too. Throw you into the woods with a backpack and make you live off the land and find your way home."

"Okay…" I looked at Sage, worried for her, and now for myself, although that was quite similar to what I was doing now. It was not lost on me how casually everyone assumed I was going to become Sawyer's wife. I mean…he had to ask me and I had to say yes. Which I totally obviously would after some hardcore groveling from Sawyer for wearing that stupid necklace and picking Meredith.

Walsh shrugged. "Clearly it's come in handy, so we have to prepare for anything."

"The Paladins do it too, I heard," Sage piped in, and my entire body froze.

"Do what?" My breath was barely a whisper.

"Their alphas go off into the woods on a survival trip or something. I heard my dad talk about it once," she said.

This was what my mom must have been talking about when Run disappeared when he was seventeen and she didn't see him for four years. It couldn't have been a four-year survival trip...right?

Walsh stood, rubbing sleep from his eyes. "I'm gonna take a two-second shower. Be ready to start walking when I get out. I want to cover the entire territory today if we can. I'm going to try to get us some horses."

Then he disappeared into the bathroom and I spun on Sage.

"Tell me everything," I whispered.

She grinned. "I don't know what you're talking about."

I smacked her arm. "Come on. I've been shot and nearly eaten by a dark fey, you owe me something happy. I saw you two kissing." I raised one eyebrow.

She peered over her coffee cup at the closed shower door and gave me a smirk. "It's been a tense couple days trying to find you. We spent one night cutting across the Wild Lands and it was so freezing we had to share a sleeping bag to keep warm."

I pumped my fist in the air. "Yes."

She burst into peals of laughter. "The chemistry is there, but I feel like when we get back to Wolf City, he'll go back to being my cousin's lead guard and my fellow coworker and we won't be anything romantic."

I frowned. "Is it against the rules or something? To date someone on your own security team."

She shook her head. "It's against *his* rules."

Just then the door handle turned and we both quieted.

Walsh stepped out of the bathroom with slicked-back wet hair. Damn, he wasn't kidding about the two-second shower. He turned and looked at me. "Demi, I'd like you to travel today with your wolf out. I think it's safer for many reasons."

Many reasons…

"Okay." At the mere thought, my wolf surged to the surface and climbed out of my skin, solidifying beside me.

"That will never not be cool…and weird," Sage commented, and I just smiled, reaching out to pet my wolf behind the ears.

"How's your shoulder?" Walsh knelt beside me and I turned to give him my back.

"It actually feels a ton better." It wasn't a hundred percent but didn't feel like it did last night.

He poked it a few times and there was a deep throb like you'd have with a bad bruise, but nothing sharp and horrible. "Looks good. No infection, and it's closing up. Those stitches will dissolve on their own."

Sage slipped on her walking boots and started to tighten the straps on her pack. "One of the deer furs has blood on it so we had to burn it, but I found this." Sage handed me a long black cloak.

I took it, nodding my thanks. "I'll just freshen up and be right out."

After going pee and brushing my teeth with a toothbrush Sawyer had packed for me, I draped the long black cloak over my shoulders and slipped into my new Converse shoes.

'These shoes are too clean. I feel bad wearing them,' I told Sawyer.

I felt him stir through our bond, but he didn't respond. He was probably still sleeping.

I stepped out of the bathroom and Walsh helped secure my pack in a way that didn't press on my healing shoulder. He'd slung one strap over my good shoulder and then tied the rest around my waist.

"You still have that fey blade from last night?" he asked. "I saw you keep it."

I nodded and tapped my pack.

"Good. It might come in handy," was all he said. With that, we doused our fire and bid our little cabin goodbye. Walsh handed us each rations for breakfast that were dismal compared to how hungry I was, but I didn't want to complain, so I thanked him and ate the peanut butter crackers.

"Why don't we just cut back through the Wild

Lands?" I asked. If they'd done it before, maybe it wasn't as dangerous as I thought.

Walsh and Sage both shared a look before he shook his head. "Let's just say our time there was not as quiet as we hoped, and we definitely alerted them to our presence. They will have the borders locked down and heavily guarded."

Damn.

"Can we get a car?" I hadn't walked this much in my life. I just wanted to be back with my mom and Raven and Sawyer.

Walsh nodded. "They use cars in Light Fey City. I can boost us one when we get there."

Boost one...aka steal. Whatever got us home quicker, I would turn the other cheek, but that meant we had to get through Dark Fey Territory first.

"So we'll try to get horses while here?" Sage asked him. He nodded, pulling a laminated map from inside of his deer skin cloak. When he opened it in front of us, I gasped. It was like the map Marmal had given me but... so much more detailed and modern. It looked like it had been inkjet printed and then laminated; it had little icons for major buildings. He pointed to a little barn icon inside of Dark Fey Territory. "Our insider said this area has animals for purchase. A man named Trip runs the trades."

Trip? Sounded shady. Like a fey drug dealer or something.

Sage looked skeptical. "A dark fey is going to sell us three horses?"

Walsh placed the map back in his jacket pocket. "A man named Trip does some illegal animal trading and will do whatever we want for the right price."

The words *illegal animal trading* made my skin crawl. I loved animals, more than people, and if this bastard had a little pet monkey in a cage or something I was totes breaking it free.

"You think that's where they got the bear?" Sage looked at the three long gashes on her arm, which were healing nicely, and Walsh nodded once.

My wolf was walking apace beside us, and Walsh glanced at her now. "All dark fey seem to have a familiar or animal that they magically bind themselves to in an effort to be more powerful or on even playing ground with our kind. Like you, Demi, they walk beside their animals yet share one mind."

Whoa. That gave me a wild idea... Maybe the Paladin magic wasn't witch in nature...maybe it was dark fey. I shivered at the thought and shoved it deep down inside of me but said nothing.

"What insider?" I asked Walsh, "You said before an insider helped you with this map."

Walsh sighed. "Few people pass through these lands and live to tell about it. Eugene did, early on in his years as an alpha guard. He's been really helpful with the knowledge we will need to make it home."

Sage stopped, what seemed like a light bulb moment hitting her. "Sawyer...his kidnapping...when he was young. I remember Eugene was the one that brought him back. The dark fey took him! Not the Paladin?"

Walsh looked at Sage and I, seemingly to calculate how much he should say. "It's classified."

Sage frowned and my heart sank. Did someone lie and tell everyone in Wolf City that the Paladins had kidnapped Sawyer when in reality it was the dark fey? That was messed up. Poor Sawyer. Being kidnapped at five years old when he was old enough to remember... what kind of scars did Sawyer carry from that?

"No offense, but why didn't Eugene come with you?" I missed the big guy hulking around campus.

Walsh and Sage shared another look. "He's currently fighting for his life in the ICU. How much has Sawyer told you about the fight that went down?"

I stumbled over my feet and nearly fell. *Fighting for his life!* "The fight with the vampires and Locke? Not much."

Walsh walked a few paces before looking back at me. "When we crossed the border to look for you in Vampire City, they were ready. They had Locke there as witness that we were trespassing."

I stepped over a fallen log and growled. "Even though I told Sawyer the vampires took me?"

Sage sighed. "How is Sawyer going to explain that you guys can talk into each other's minds? No one believed him. Said he was trying to mess with the murder investigation and that you ran off because you were upset he picked Meredith."

Anger surged up inside of me. "Wait, so no one believes I was kidnapped? They all think I ran away?"

Sage rubbed the back of her neck. "You packed a bag, you took your phone, people saw you running through campus crying."

Fuck, I had no idea that Sawyer was the only one who believed me.

"Your testimony is the only thing that can prove the vampires kidnapped you," Sage said.

My mind spun. "So...what happened when Locke wouldn't let Sawyer look for me?" I chewed my lip thinking of what Sawyer told me about killing Locke.

Walsh gave me a side glance and a frenzied grin pulled at his face. "I've never seen Sawyer so badass."

Sage reached out and smacked his chest. "That was scary. He almost died."

My heart beat wildly as Walsh chuckled. "He wiped the floor with that fey."

We'd reached a really thick area of trees and went single file to get through them. "What happened? Tell me about the fight," I pressed.

I hated not being there with Sawyer, but I knew from seeing him kill Butcher that he was an amazing fighter.

A half smirk pulled at the corner of Sage's mouth. "The second Locke said that Sawyer would legally be unable to search the building for you, he wolfed out."

Walsh growled. "Locke went nuts, like a wild dark fey. His eyes turned black and he snapped, attacking Sawyer."

Oh my gosh. "What else happened!" I rushed to keep up with them as we traipsed through the thick trees. There was an opening ahead, and Walsh stopped and faced me.

His eyes were threaded with yellow. "He grabbed Sawyer's wolf by the neck and lifted him into the air, told his father that if any of us made one more move it would be an act of *war*."

My hands went to my face, covering my mouth.

Sage grinned. "So Sawyer bit his hand and tore it clean off."

My mouth went dry. Holy shit, that man had a temper.

Walsh nodded. "And everything erupted into chaos. Sawyer killed Locke, but we had to retreat. There were too many of them and we weren't prepared. Eugene protected the alpha with his life, as is his duty, and here we are."

Oh no. So they tried to hurt Sawyer's dad too? Poor Eugene.

All of this…because of me. Shame burned my cheeks as I thought about what would have happened if I hadn't run off, if I—

"Stop it." Sage pointed a finger at me. "The vampires have been doing this for years. My uncle is just too soft. Sawyer won't stand for it. It's been a long time coming.

It's time someone stood up to their corruption and evil deeds."

I swallowed hard and nodded. Hard to think of it that way but—

We heard voices just up ahead as Walsh put his finger to his lips in a sign of quiet.

The voices were speaking a weird language I didn't know, and I reached out and brushed my fingers over the top of my wolf's head to calm her.

Walsh silently pulled out his map, pointed to the barn, and then up ahead to the clearing with a thumbs-up.

The barn was just up ahead.

When the voice passed, Walsh looked at Sage and I, chewing his lip as if wrestling with what to do.

"Don't even think about going in there alone!" Sage whisper-screamed.

He sighed. "I don't want you guys to get hurt if things go south."

Sage growled, "I'm not a fragile princess in need of saving." Her teeth gritted together as her jaw clenched. Then she pointed to me. "She's more powerful than both of us combined. Her wolf can walk through walls. So don't start with me."

He blanched at the knowledge my wolf could do that and gave her an appraising look, which she returned with a wolfish grin.

"Fine. But if things go south, run," he agreed.

"Not on your life." Sage put a hand on her hip.

I nodded to my wolf and tapped my chest. "I should probably have her join me."

"No." Walsh reached out and stopped me. "I had you keep her out for a reason. If you were to get angry or need to fight, and they saw her come out of you, they would know what you are."

Truth.

"But if we walk in with a wolf, they will definitely know we are from Wolf City," I said.

Walsh nodded. "They'll be able to smell it either way. Better we look like four wolf shifters than two werewolves and one..." He looked at me. "Split shifter?"

I shrugged. "Better than *demon*."

Sage nodded. "You're right. Own what we are and say we're on the run? We were banished?"

Walsh shook his head. "*You* will say nothing. I will do the talking. I'm hoping to flash enough gold at this guy that he doesn't even blink at my request for transport animals."

Sage crossed her arms and glared at him but nodded. It was clear he outranked her or whatever.

He handed Sage the map. "In case we get separated." And then he pulled his sword and lay it on the ground, covering it with leaves. "Hide the weapons. Eugene said they take them and don't give them back."

Great. I reached down, scraped some of the fallen leaves and dirt away, and then deposited the shotgun Marmal had given me and the fey blade, covering it. I'd grown fond of the weapon and hoped it wouldn't be stolen while we were in this place.

Walsh looked at me. "Your name is Jessica. Understood?"

Okay, wow, so we were really paranoid. I nodded.

After that, we stepped out into the clearing and my eyes immediately were drawn to a giant pole barn. It was huge, must have been two hundred feet long by a hundred feet wide. Maybe for racing animals or keeping them in there or something. There was a chimney at the top that spewed dark smoke, and the scent that hit my nose was so confusing, I actually scrunched up my face.

Fox, beaver, bear, tiger, rat, and magic. *So* much magic...

This place was crawling with magic and smelled like a zoo. A crazy combination for sure. As we approached, my eyes ran over a large dude about Eugene's size. He stood like a sentinel at the front of two large double doors; his forehead and nose were troll-like, as were the tiny delicate tusks that protruded from his cheeks, but he had slightly pointy ears and black eyes. He didn't look a full-blown fey; they were tall and willowy and had *really* pointy ears. He was somewhere between a troll and a fey.

"Ithaki," Sage whispered to me, and my eyes widened.

Shit. I hoped he didn't know who I was from the day Sawyer killed their leader.

What was an Ithaki doing in Dark Fey Territory? A troll-fey one no less? Did he live here? I was slightly horrified and intrigued by this.

The man inhaled through his nose and growled. "Wolf."

Walsh produced a small gold coin from his pocket, legit gold, and handed it to the man. "I need to speak with Trip."

The man looked at us like we were the scum of the earth, his eyes even roaming over my wolf before he looked back at Walsh and tapped his palm.

Walsh produced another gold coin and it clinked with the first one. The giant put them in his pocket and stepped aside, allowing us entry into the building. We walked past him quickly and into a barrage of sounds and smells.

A stone sank in my gut as my eyes ran across the hundreds of cages that lined the far walls of the large barn. Racoons, foxes, dogs, cats, every kind of animal you could think of. I tucked into Walsh's side as my wolf pressed against my other side and Sage brought up the rear. Seeing so many caged and mistreated animals had us all shrinking together in our own little pack. I skidded to a stop, causing Sage to run into my back as my eyes stopped on a stall that was barred like a jail cell. Thick iron bars went from the floor to the ceiling, encasing the most magnificent creature I'd ever seen.

"Is that...?" My mouth dropped open. The most

beautiful pearl-colored dragon stood in the center of the cell, her turquoise eyes tracking me as I tried to walk closer to her. Walsh's hand snaked out and grasped my upper arm as he yanked me back. I could tell by Sage's wide eyes that she also didn't think dragons existed before this very moment.

I started to look at the other cages and stalls more closely now. Horses, buffalo, every animal looked "normal" but they all smelled of magic.

"Holy drago—"

Walsh shushed me, forcing us to all start moving again and I had to bite my tongue from freaking out.

"Mods," Sage whispered to me as we followed Walsh deeper into the center of the room, where some crowd was shouting and chanting.

"Mods?" I looked confused.

She gestured to the animals in the other cages. "Modified animals. They're given magic powers before they're bound to the fey. They probably use the dragon to do it."

Holy shifter.

I looked back at the dragon, sad to see the brokenness in her eyes, the same brokenness I once recognized in Sawyer and in myself. My wolf whimpered and I knew exactly what she meant. The cages were too small and all of the animals looked mistreated. This place was a nightmare and I'd wished we'd never come.

One by one, the crowd of people parted, craning

their necks to stare at us, nostrils flaring. The room was ninety percent made up of dark fey with long, inky-black hair and sharp pointy ears. But I also spotted trolls, vampires, and a few witches. This was clearly some kind of black-market trading post that was open to all races...except for ours. Wolves stuck together mostly. Pack over everything else. I pulled the hood higher over my face and remembered my name was Jessica.

Walsh boldly walked us through the crowd until I saw why there was a crowd at all. In the center of the barn was a...fighting ring. A cage sat in the middle of the room and my stomach sank when I saw the dead form of a fey man lying in the center of it. A giant troll loomed over him, snarling, black blood dripping from his mouth.

The crowd erupted into cheers just as a dark fey man in a sleek charcoal suit turned to look at us. His eyes flicked quickly from Walsh, to Sage, to me, before lingering on my wolf.

He simply nodded his head to the back of the barn and then walked away.

Walsh gave us a distressing look and we followed.

This had to be Trip, and luring us into a back corner of the barn wasn't my idea of safe and fun. We passed more cages, and I *did* spot a small monkey, causing a whimper to die in my throat. I'd always wanted a pet monkey. I told my mom when I was twelve that if she didn't get me one, I'd run away. She didn't get me one, and I never ran away, but dammit I'd wanted to. Now I realized the irony here, that a pet monkey would have been stolen from their parents and kept in a cage just like this one.

When we reached the corner of the barn, the man opened a hidden door in the wall and stepped inside. Walsh hesitated a moment and gave me a look. It was a look that said, *If we get jumped, I need you to be a badass and flex those freaky powers.* I nodded. I didn't yet know the full extent of my powers, but I could feel my wolf thrumming with anticipation. Walsh stepped through the door first and looked left and right quickly, before moving more fully inside. We followed him in and I left the door open for easy escape.

The office was tiny, which was made all the more uncomfortable by the fact that the man at the desk lit up a giant cigar, puffing a few times before it started smoking. Behind him stood two giant troll-fey Ithaki. The two huge dudes stood over seven feet tall and had scars all over their faces. One of them who had a dyed purple mohawk had a seriously broken nose; it bulged and protruded oddly. They were ugly as sin, but looked like his most prized fighters.

The man, Trip I assumed, had paper-thin white skin, peppered with black veins. His long, dark hair hung halfway down his back and my gaze flew to his black-painted fingernails. This guy was like an emo goth dark fey. Quite a character.

"What can I do for you fine wolves?" he purred.

I didn't like or trust him.

"You Trip?" Walsh asked.

The man just nodded, once.

Walsh produced a small bag of gold coins, palming them and holding them out to Trip. "I need a horse and carriage or any other type of animal that can get me across the fey realm quickly."

Trip grinned and I tried not to wince at his yellow tobacco-stained teeth. He took the gold from Walsh, peeked inside the velvet bag and chuckled. "This isn't enough for what you want."

Walsh growled. "That's *more* than enough."

Trip stood, inhaling a deep drag of his cigar, and puffed it out in Walsh's face. "Before the war, yes. But this morning I got an order from the dark fey king to deliver all of my riding animals and carriages to prepare for war."

Holy shit. Prepare for war? With us?

I kept my face a mask of calm as Trip looked at me, gaze narrowing as he tried to peer inside of my pulled-up hood. "She looks a bit familiar," he commented, and I had to refrain from lowering my head to hide because that would be shady.

Walsh stepped in front of me, ignoring his comment.

He pointed to the gold. "There must be something you can give me for this."

Trip sneered, looking Walsh up and down like he was a specimen. "What are four pretty little wolves doing so far from home anyway? Dodging the war?" His gaze turned skeptical.

Had a full-on war broken out or just this little tiff with the vampires? Now I was nervous. I'd need to check in with Sawyer when I had time.

Walsh nodded. "Can you help us?"

He looked back at his two troll guards, who nodded. Turning back to face Walsh, he clasped his hands together. "I'll give you one horse and buggy if you win your fight."

I saw Sage tighten next to me at the same time that I did.

"Fight?" Sage growled.

The man's gaze snapped to hers and he grinned. "We haven't had a female fighter in ages. Would love if—"

"No." Walsh's command was laced with his wolf, and even though I wasn't facing him, I knew his eyes would be yellow.

Trip grinned as Walsh dropped his deer skin and pulled off his shirt, showcasing a lean, muscular back full of small scars.

"I'll fight. Then you give us the horse and carriage. Do I have your word?"

Trip's upper lip curled at that and I wondered if there was something to a fey giving you his word, because he seemed reluctant to do so.

"If you win your fight, you have my word that you may leave with the horse and carriage I assign you."

Walsh looked at me and Sage. "Say it again and include them."

Trip chortled. "Smart boy. If you win your fight, you have my *word* that you may leave with these three lovely ladies *and* the horse and carriage I assign you."

Walsh nodded, seemingly satisfied with that and it took me a moment to realize the *three* ladies included my wolf. He thought she was a werewolf in wolf form. Good.

I could tell from the look on Sage's face that she wanted to beg Walsh not to fight, but she kept quiet as we left the office.

"You can warm up over there." Trip indicated to a corner of the room and we all followed his gaze. My stomach dropped when I noticed the wolf inside of the cage near a red foam practice mat. She was panting, licking at an injured paw and whimpering. I inhaled deeply and smelled a female Paladin wolf. She had an earthy smell, like Arrow, wolf shifter but also uniquely Paladin. I could smell the human on her too.

There was no way we could leave her here.

Walsh met my gaze and shook his head, knowing what I was thinking.

"We'll be taking her too. Name your price," I told Trip as he turned to walk away. The Paladin wolf must have heard that, because her yellow eyes snapped up to meet mine and I held her gaze for a long moment.

He spun on his heel and followed my line of sight to

the Paladin wolf and then grinned. Those yellow stained teeth made me shudder.

Walsh's hand snaked out and gripped my upper arm. "No."

I met his yellow gaze. "Yes," I growled.

"She's not one of us," he snipped back to me, barely a whisper.

I yanked my arm from his, feeling too conflicted to explain. "I'm *not* leaving without her. You saw how the Paladin man tried to save me after my fall. *This* is fucked up." I pointed to the cage.

Walsh's face fell then, and he swallowed hard. There was a human in there, a shifter, not just an animal. He was there when I fell, he knew the Paladin man tried to help me.

"That pretty thing will get me a fair price at market. She can birth future Ithaki," Trip told us.

What? They had an Ithaki *breeding program?* I shivered and my wolf peeled back her lips and snarled at the man.

'*Let me fight for her,*' my wolf said, and I nodded immediately.

"My little sister here will fight you for her," I said, gesturing to my wolf and figuring the sister thing made the most sense.

Trip looked at me like I was losing my mind before he and his henchmen burst into laughter. "You think that little pup can stand against one of my fighters?"

I opened my mouth to speak and Walsh growled, shutting me up. "We will fight doubles. Me and the wolf against two of your strongest men. If we win, we get to leave with the horse, carriage, *and* the Paladin wolf."

Trips eyes glittered. "A doubles fight?" He looked at his guards, who nodded once.

"The crowd will love it." He rubbed his chin. "All right, you have a deal. You have my word that if you win this fight, you, the ladies, and the Paladin wolf are free to go on my horse and carriage."

Walsh nodded and Trip turned and left just like that. When Trip was gone, Walsh rounded on me as Sage tucked in closer to my side. "Are you losing your mind? You probably just got us both killed. Now I'm going to have to fight two of them while protecting you!" he growled.

I scowled at him. "Are you saying my wolf is useless?"

She growled to let him know how much she resented that thought.

He softened, his shoulders slumping. "No, but she's not trained. Sage would have been a better bet, and all of your powers are tied up in your human form. This could be a *total* disaster."

I frowned. Was he right? I mean, I could walk through walls, but that wasn't going to do me any good here. Not to mention it would get my special gifts outed.

Sage gave me a sidelong glance. "Why on earth would you stick up for a Paladin wolf? They are responsible for the constant attacks on Wolf City and my family."

She didn't even know about the curse. If she did, she would feel even worse about the Paladins, but I didn't know those Paladins. I couldn't lie any longer and I didn't want to. They had the wrong idea about the Paladins and I wanted to set them straight.

"Because I'm one of them. A Paladin." I held my chin high as Sage's eyes went wide and Walsh's lips turned into a frown of confusion.

Nothing like dropping a truth bomb right before a fight to your death.

CHAPTER SEVEN

OLY SHIT, YOUR MOM BANGED A PALADIN!" SAGE
whisper-screamed.

Eww, *banged?* I didn't want to think of my mom
and that word ever again. Something else to talk to my
future therapist about. I quickly caught Walsh and Sage
up to speed on everything about my mom's affair with
Run, and Sage was freaking out, while Walsh was eerily
calm.

"Walsh. He *helped* me. That old Paladin man who
found me at the base of the mountain. You *saw* it."

He sighed, and the crowd cheered behind us. They
must have just announced our fight.

"I don't know what I saw, okay." He rubbed his
forehead. "Look, we'll take the wolf and let her go
outside of town, but that's it. She can't go the entire way
to the Witch Lands with us, I won't allow it."

I nodded, grateful for anything he would give me.

"And we will be taking the dragon too, right?" Sage gave him puppy dog eyes and popped out her bottom lip.

He smirked. "Not on your life."

Then he looked back at me. "No offense. But do you even know how to fight as a wolf?"

Ouch. Offense taken but... "Not really."

'I'll rip out all of their throats before they can even blink,' my wolf, my voice, said in my head, and I turned to her and raised one eyebrow.

Okay...so she was confident.

He gave a long-suffering sigh and pulled off his shirt once more, showcasing his muscles. "If you die, then Sawyer's going to kill me."

"Then I won't die," I promised him, and my wolf nodded for good measure.

Walsh knelt down and looked my wolf in the eyes before looking back up at me. "When I'm in wolf form, will I be talking to her or you or...?"

I chuckled. "Her, but also me. We're one. Pretty much." Okay, I think I just confused myself.

Walsh frowned for a moment, but then nodded.

"We're ready!" Trip called from behind us as the crowd began to gather in a tight circle. There was a giant wad of money in Trip's hand, colored bills I didn't recognize, and golden coins.

Walsh gave us his back as he dropped his pants and then his boxers and I looked away to give him privacy, but I noticed Sage's gaze flick downward for a half second.

I grinned and she turned to face me with red cheeks. "Shut up," she mouthed.

Walsh was on all fours now, his wolf staring mine down.

'Demi?' he asked.

My attention went to my wolf and she nodded.

'I'm ready,' my wolf told him.

He padded over to the fighting arena and I followed in wolf form.

'We fight as a team. One unit.' Walsh's wolf's voice was gruff and calculated. You could tell his head was already in the fight. My wolf nodded and he went on. *'If I clamp down on one of their wrists, it means I'm going to pin him down so you can rip out his throat. Can you do that?'*

Fear surged through my human half, but my wolf was unfazed. *'Yes,'* she replied simply.

'If I go left, you go right. We need to keep their attention divided and take them down one by one.'

Again, my wolf nodded. I tapped into her feelings and was shocked to feel nothing. Not one ounce of fear. If anything she was...bloodthirsty. She looked at the cages holding the animals and I understood. She wanted revenge for this, for keeping all of the animals in cages, experimenting on them and selling them.

The crowd grew louder as Walsh and my wolf

approached and he stopped and looked at her. *'I don't know what powers your wolf has, but I don't want to see them out there. If you show that you are anything but an ordinary werewolf, you'll be in a cage. Got it?'*

I could feel rebellion rise up in my wolf, but she nodded.

She respected Walsh and would listen to him.

Trip grinned, opening the large fighter cage, and I let my gaze fall on the two giants inside of it. The same ones from the office. I took time to really appraise them now. They were massive, the size of a full-grown bear, but they were definitely Ithaki. Half troll and half... dark fey?

My stomach tightened as I had a wild thought: what would happen if my wolf died? Would I die too? We were connected, but also apart, so I really had no idea and I didn't want to find out now. We stepped into the large fifty-foot square cage and stood in front of the giant troll-fey Ithaki.

"Place all final bets!" Trip shouted to the crowd as Walsh bared his lips and growled at the purple mohawk Ithaki.

'You need to mentally psych them out. Show them you aren't weak,' Walsh coached my wolf.

Without warning, she tipped her head back and let out the most spine-chilling howl I'd ever heard. It was deep and long and gut wrenching. Suddenly the Paladin in its cage right behind us howled back, and then Walsh joined in. Soon all of the animals in the room started to go nuts. Horses, monkeys, even the dragon all made agitated sounds and shook the doors of their cages.

Trip's face fell, marred with shock at the disruption my wolf's howl had caused in his animals, and so did the two Ithaki's.

My wolf had some kind of effect on all the animals…I could *feel* it. She had a connection to them.

Whatever she'd done, it had worked to mentally psych out the two trolls. When the fight bell went off, they stood there stunned, staring at my wolf as Walsh burst into the air.

'*Get behind them and start tearing at their ankles,*' Walsh told my wolf.

The troll-Ithaki went from staring at my wolf like idiots to craning their necks at the werewolf flying directly at their faces. The troll on the left was slightly taller and redheaded, while the one on the right had the purple mohawk and looked more fey-like. Walsh went for the redhead and I remembered his instructions.

We attack as a team.

I darted between the troll's legs and went right for Red's ankle as Walsh had commanded. Taking the back of his heel into my mouth, I clamped down until my teeth sank deep into warm flesh, and then tore my jaws away, yanking out tendons and muscle.

A roar of pain filled the space and I stepped out of the way just in time for the Ithaki to fall forward in pain. He crashed against the mat, practically shaking the walls of the barn with his fall, lying helplessly on the ground as he held his ankle, which was bleeding a dark greenish black.

Whoa. That was awesome—

The crowd went wild.

Thin rivulets of the greenish blood trickled onto the dirt-packed floor as the injured troll made a fist and aimed for me. I turned to run but was too slow. His knuckles crashed into my ribs and the wind knocked right out of me. I padded across the cage wheezing, trying to get a lungful of air.

That bastard.

Walsh was circling the redhead, taking nips of his flesh here and there, weakening him, when my wolf bared her teeth and charged forward to finish him off.

'Look out!' Walsh cried but it was too late. Giant fingers dug into my fur as I'd forgotten all about Mr. Mohawk. I was yanked up into the air by the skin of my back, and tight pain seared across my fur as my skin pulled taut.

A howl ripped from my throat and the crowd went wild.

My jaws snapped left and right but couldn't reach the douchebag's arm. I was like a little yipping chihuahua to this guy. He pulled me close to his face and inhaled. I was still too far to bite him though, so it only served to piss me off.

"You smell like magic," he cooed and I gulped. "What a tasty treat you will make."

My stomach sank as he opened his mouth, showcasing glistening pointed teeth, and started to shove me inside like he was eating a very large burrito.

I blinked and suddenly I was watching the fight from my human perspective. Terror ripped through me as I saw that Walsh was locked in battle with the redheaded troll and my wolf was about to be eaten. Pressure built between my shoulders and inside my chest until I felt like I might burst.

"No!" I shouted and thrust my hands out. An unseen force flew from my palms. I willed it to slam into the troll, to force him to drop my wolf.

And it did.

The troll's eyes went wide as he was thrown back into the wall of the cage. One by one, his fingers lifted away from my wolf slowly as if he were fighting it. He grunted against the force, until finally my wolf was free and dropped to the ground. The air felt thick with my power, and I wasn't the only one who'd noticed. Sage looked at me wide-eyed as the crowd started to murmur and look around for the cause of the magical force.

Just then, Walsh, who had been in a ground grapple with Red, slipped away from the troll, and the crowd seemed to shrug off the magical incident.

I was back in my wolf's perspective, looking through her eyes and up at a very angry Mr. Mohawk. Rolling to avoid his kick, I decided to help out Walsh and avoid Mohawk as long as I could. Turning, I scrambled across the cage and wiggled under Red. His hand came down, about to grab Walsh, and I bit into his wrist, pinning it down with the move Walsh told me about. Walsh reacted with the lithe grace of a cheetah. Springing from his position on the ground, he leapt and attached himself to Red's jugular with his teeth. With one yank, Walsh came away with his jugular and the crowd went insane.

The redheaded troll-fey's hand that I held in my jaw went completely limp as he bled out, sticky green-black blood pooling around him in a rapidly growing puddle.

The cheers of the crowd reached a crescendo while I spun to keep my eye on Mr. Mohawk troll. He stood right behind me, grinning, holding a twelve-inch hunting knife in one hand, and my heart dropped into my stomach like a stone.

No weapons were allowed. Someone must have handed it to him and no one said a thing.

Awesome.

'*He's got a knife, I'm shifting to human,*' Walsh said. '*I'll grapple him to the ground and you finish him.*'

My wolf nodded as Walsh started to shift.

Suddenly Sage was there, tossing him sweatpants, which he slipped on quickly. The troll-fey waited patiently, grinning at us the entire time. He looked like he was going to enjoy this part and it made me sick.

I inhaled, the scent of hot wires reaching my nose.

'*I don't like this. It smells wrong... The blade isn't normal,*' I told Walsh.

He didn't say anything, and it took me too long to realize it was because he was human now and could no longer hear my wolf.

Shit.

Mohawk held the knife like he knew what he was doing, and my heart jumped into my throat with panic. I didn't like the sickly green color that shimmered on the edge of the blade.

Magic.

'*Tell him it's a magic blade,*' my wolf said to my human half.

I forgot that I had a human half that could speak. Just as the troll lunged for Walsh, I screamed, "Magic blade!" as my wolf bared her teeth and growled inside of the cage. The knife skated past Walsh's skin as he arched his back to dodge it. Pivoting, he then pulled up his fists and rained blow after blow onto the troll-fey's face and chest, wherever Walsh could reach. It was like watching a tortured pit bull backed into a corner. Walsh was attacking like he had completely gone berserk and caught the troll off guard. But I knew that wouldn't last long.

My wolf crouched and then sprang, aiming for the troll's throat. He saw me coming, briefly taking his eyes off of Walsh, and lunged for me, knife drawn high. It was like time stopped. I could tell he was going to stab me in the ribcage. But I was going too fast, with too much momentum, to slow down at this point. All I could do was brace for impact.

But the slice of pain never came. In a blur a motion, Walsh leapt in front of my wolf, knocking her to the side and out of harm's way. His shoulder jammed so hard into my ribs, I lost my breath as I was thrown to the ground. The troll's knife slid into Walsh's stomach like he was cutting butter, and a howl ripped from my wolf's throat at the same time that my human half screamed.

"Walsh!" Sage tore across the dirt-packed floor and gripped the iron cage with her fingers.

Walsh let out a strangled cry, crumpling to the ground with a look of absolute agony on his face, holding an open wound that was slowly trickling crimson.

The troll-fey grinned, adjusting his grip on the knife as he looked at Walsh like he was a rare steak about to be carved.

Over my dead fucking body.

Sage's head whipped back to my human half. "*Do something.*"

My wolf stood, shaking herself as unbridled rage consumed the both of us. Mohawk bent, ignoring my wolf, and hovered over Walsh, giving me a nice view of his lumpy ass. Two lumps of flesh bulged out between his legs, straining under the fabric of his pants.

My human half winced at what was about to happen, but my wolf had no such displeasure. Flesh was flesh.

I leapt, opening my jaws, and the room took in a

133

collective gasp. When I felt the bulk of his skin and muscle in my mouth, I clamped down.

Hard.

One ball-less, mohawked troll-fey, coming right up.

I shook my jaws like a dog trying to break the neck of his favorite stuffed toy, and the flesh came away cleanly, along with the cloth of his pants.

An inhuman howl cut through the barn; the knife dropped to the floor with a clatter and the troll shook violently, falling over to the side and passing out. When he went completely limp, I spat the flesh from my mouth and didn't wait for the giant to get up. This mother-fucker brought a knife to a fist fight.

That meant prison rules, bitch.

His waxy skin glistened with sweat as I pounced on his chest and peered down at him. The crowd chanted with an insane fervor.

Wolf! Wolf! Wolf!

I glanced over at Walsh, eyelids lowering as he got weaker and weaker, and knew that I needed to end this quickly so that we could get him help.

But my wolf hesitated.

I couldn't kill someone when they were defenseless and knocked out cold. Right? I turned back to look at Trip. His eyes were glittering with malice. Could he call off the fight? Or was death the only way out of this cage? I probably should have asked that before—

A firm grip wrapped around my throat and squeezed

so hard that my windpipe felt like it was crushed into a fine powder. I turned to look at the troll-fey, eyes wide, and was met with the most horrifying black eyes I'd ever seen.

"You fucking *bitch*!" he snarled, spittle flying from his mouth and onto my muzzle. He panted, no doubt in a world of pain, but that didn't seem to stop him from having a vise-like grip on my throat. My wolf bucked backward, trying to struggle out of his grasp, but it was no use. He was too strong, and I was in a shitty position with no footholds or anything I could use to my advantage. With his other hand, he reached to the side, patting the mat of the cage wildly, no doubt looking for the knife. I panicked, unable to breathe and starting to feel weak.

"I'm going to dissect you, organ by organ, and when I'm done you won't—" He froze, looking up as a shadow passed over his face.

I was starting to see spots, blackness dancing at the edges of my vision. I needed air. *Now.* My wolf wanted to turn ghostly, to disappear from his fingers and go spectral, but it would out what I was to everyone.

'*Hang on,*' my human half said, and I blinked, shifting to her vision.

"Looking for this?" Walsh grunted, knife in hand as he stood over the troll. The beast was lying flat on his back, groin area bleeding freely with my wolf on top of his chest.

He released my wolf immediately, trying to scramble

upward, when Walsh dropped to one knee and sliced his throat quickly and cleanly.

My wolf pulled in deep, ragged gasps of air as the troll-fey went limp.

The crowd went wild, some booing and others cheering, all while my shifter healing repaired my crushed trachea or whatever he'd done. The lump in my throat became less painful, and I was soon able to breathe normally. Money exchanged hands as Trip glared at Walsh and I through the bars.

We'd no doubt just killed two of his prize fighters, but he gave his word. That had to mean something. When everyone was paid, he walked over to us, holding a wad of gold coins in his pocket.

"I believe you owe us our payment now, sir?" Sage said boldly, glancing at Walsh and my wolf nervously as we limped out of the cage, which had just been unlocked. Walsh held on to his bleeding ribcage, but a thin, steady stream of blood exited out his fingers.

"My word is good," he growled. "Fetch the horse," he snapped to one of his lackeys. I could tell by the bulge of coins in his pocket that he could buy more of whatever he wanted.

I cleared my throat. "And release the Paladin wolf."

He sneered at me through eyes blacker than oil. "And that."

———•·•———

Ten minutes later, I knelt over Walsh's limp and bleeding form as he clutched his side in pain. The Paladin wolf was curled in a ball at my feet. When Trip had unlocked her cage, she'd cowered in the corner, shaking. Sage tried to sweetly coo her out but it didn't work. With Walsh near death, I'd grown impatient, and only when I put my hand out and commanded in a firm voice for to her to come to me did she move. She hadn't shifted to her human form and I was okay with that, because we had Walsh to worry about first.

Walsh groaned and my hands shook as I rummaged through the med-kit Sawyer had sent for something that looked useful. A whimper of desperation left my throat, and the Paladin at my feet curled tighter around my legs in response. I frowned, looking down at her while my wolf sat at the back of the carriage we were in and watched all of us with inquisitive eyes. We were supposed to ditch the Paladin at the end of the road ahead, but something wasn't right with her. She was too meek, she'd be eaten by a coyote at this rate, and definitely taken by a dark fey. Besides, Sage was too focused on Walsh to even think about her family's sworn enemy at my ankles.

Sage rode in the front of the eighteenth-century stagecoach, holding the horse's reins as it galloped along the dusty dirt-packed road and through the woods. "Should I try to stitch him up? Why isn't he healing!" I asked, grasping a suture kit. Walsh's eyes were fluttering open, closed, open, closed. I'd told Sage to get us away from the barn in case anyone tried to retaliate for what we'd done. Trip kept his word and let us go, but that didn't mean he wouldn't have someone chase us.

She shook her head. "Stitches won't help if it's internal. That blade smelled like magic because it was. The magic disables our rapid healing." Her voice cracked and I let a curse word fly. "Just keep pressure on it until I can get him to a healer fey."

My eyes bugged. Light fey were healer fey, and Sawyer said they were currently *not* our allies. They were also in the next territory over. We didn't have that kind of time.

"Light fey aren't in our alliance anymore," I reminded her, watching as tears rolled down her cheeks.

I could see her jaw clench shut, her beautiful face marred with dust and determination and a whole lotta panic. "We don't have any other options. He'll bleed out before I get him to the Witch Lands."

"He'll bleed out before we get out of this territory!" I shouted, hoping my bestie would see reason. I didn't want to be the only one making the hard decisions here, but I *would* shove a hot metal rod poker into his wound in a minute if I had to. I had to do something. I wouldn't just let him die without trying.

Leaning down, careful not to put a knee on the Paladin wolf wound around my leg or my injured friend, I peeled Walsh's hand away from his stomach and choked on a half sob when sticky dark blood bubbled out. The last bit of consciousness left him then and his eyes rolled into the back of his head before his whole body went limp.

"No!" I shouted in a strangled cry. Why did I do that? I was just trying to assess the damage. He'd gotten stabbed saving my dumb ass, I couldn't let him die.

"STOP!" I shouted to Sage. The jerky ride wasn't doing us any favors, and we were far enough away now that we had some good distance between us and the barn. She looked back, saw Walsh's unconscious form and paled, yanking the reins. We skidded to a jerky stop, and by instinct I stuck two fingers into the hole in his belly, grimacing at the wet, warm flesh that swallowed my digits.

"Don't you fucking die on me, Walsh," I growled. My wolf stepped up next to my side, pressing into me, and then went semitransparent. Without question, I needed to be whole for this. I couldn't even think straight right now; having my wolf with me might help. She jumped up, crashing into my chest as the Paladin wolf at my feet watched us with searing yellow eyes.

A thought struck me then. We had a med-kit...*and* Sawyer was premed.

'Sawyer, Walsh has been stabbed in the gut. We have a med-kit. Can you walk me through saving him?'

I braced myself for his no doubt frantic reply, wondering if I was even capable of piercing his flesh and doing stitches or whatever was needed. Luckily, my fingers shoved inside of him seemed to have stopped the blood, for now.

But the reply I needed never came. Horror struck me. He didn't answer me this morning either. I'd thought he was just asleep, but now I wondered...

Oh God. Problem for future Demi. I needed to focus on Walsh now, and I was on my own.

"Open the suture kit!" I yelled to Sage, who just stood over Walsh's unconscious form and stared. The Paladin wolf at my feet whined and I wished she'd give me room, but she seemed hell-bent on sticking close to me like a damn ankle weight.

Sage's hands shook as she ripped open the suture kit I'd dropped at my feet. My mother taught me to sew a button at age twelve, so I could totally do it...

The form at my feet tightened, and I was about to nudge the wolf away when I realized she'd started shifting.

Unless she was a fucking doctor, I didn't want to have to deal with her right now. The fingers I'd stuck into Walsh's stomach to keep the blood from gushing out was grossing me out more and more by the second. I couldn't deal with one more thing.

My eyes flicked to the small naked brunette who was now crouched in a ball, head down as she barely peered at me through short, cropped bangs. I'd never seen a more fearful and submissive wolf in my life. She mumbled something softly, too soft for me to hear it, and I felt annoyed. "Speak up!" I snapped.

Walsh was going to fucking die and I was going to have to tell Sawyer he died saving me. It was all my fault and I would live with this guilt for the rest of my life.

"Do you want him healed, Alpha?" the girl said, louder this time.

My eyes flicked to Sage at the same moment hers met mine.

Alpha?

Why would she call me that? I shook myself from my thoughts, focusing on the most important part of her words.

"Yes. I do. *Very* much," I told her.

Please be a trauma surgeon.

She nodded, rubbing her hands together, which shook her breasts. She didn't seem to mind being naked, crouching over Walsh with her bare ass out for all to see. My gaze again flicked to Sage as if to say, *What the fuck was happening?*

She just shrugged, and we both looked at the timid brown-haired teen expectantly. I inhaled, trying to get a better read on her. She was definitely submissive as all hell, but I'd never smelled so much magic on one person in all my life. Now that I had a moment to think and assess her, I took another inhale, watching Sage do the same.

Hope thrummed through my chest when the coppery hot wire scent of magic hit my nostrils strong and powerful.

Was she a healer? Or was she going to stick some herbs in his gut and hope for the best?

As if reading my thoughts, she clapped her hands together loudly and blue sparks shot from her palms.

Holy shit.

Sage swallowed hard and I saw the hope in her eyes too.

The brown-haired girl looked up at me. "Please remove your fingers, Alpha. I will save him for you."

I was...stunned...again by her use of that word. It sounded so...soft and respectful on her tongue, and she sounded so sure. My heart thundered in my chest. Did she somehow know who my bio father was? Could other Paladins smell my lineage? Arrow hadn't...just because I was half of a Paladin alpha, that didn't make *me* an alpha. Right?

I looked at Sage, wondering if we should trust this girl with Walsh's life.

She gave one curt nod, and I pulled my finger out of the wet hole in his rib cage. Blood bubbled to the surface as the Paladin sighed deeply. "Father God, guide my magic," she whispered, and again Sage and I shared a look.

Please be a badass healer, please be a badass healer, please be—

Holy rattlesnake.

I gasped as blue sparks lit up her face, and Sage's, and...everything. This wasn't witch magic. This was... something else. Something breathtakingly beautiful.

Little glimmers of bright blue rained down from her palms like glittering snow and fell onto Walsh's abdomen. It coated his skin, the sticky blood, his gaping hole, his entire body, making him look like an injured alien unicorn. Walsh's entire form glowed with glittering blue as the young naked Paladin female breathed in and out deeply through her nose, with her eyes closed.

"Protect me from evil, Father," she whimpered, and I frowned just as an unseen force knocked into her and she fell backward, holding her stomach.

My eyes widened as I ran to her, forgetting all about Walsh. She lay flat on her back on the splintered wood of the carriage, looking up at the sky. Her fingers clutched her naked stomach as blood pooled around her.

"What the hell!" I shrieked, glancing back at Walsh, who gasped, taking in a deep breath as if he'd just been shocked back to life. My gaze flicked to his stomach... *completely healed.* Not even a pink mark or scar to show where he had once been injured.

How was that possible?

I grabbed the young girl—she looked barely sixteen—and took her into my arms, shaking her. "What happened!" What was that invisible force that had pushed her back? Why was she now bleeding where Walsh had just been injured? I had more questions than answers.

She looked up at the sky, smiling as if she didn't have a care in the world.

"How do I help you?" I whimpered.

Her eyes found mine and I was struck by the deepest turquoise-blue eyes I'd ever seen. They were threaded through with shafts of yellow, making them look like they contained lightning. Reaching up, she stroked my face. "Alpha."

Something stirred inside of me. My wolf? I inhaled. No. It was...something else. The scent of magic filled the air and my chest constricted. What was the point of saving one life just to take another? Had this girl just given her life for Walsh?

"Claim me," she muttered.

What?

I didn't know jack shit about the regular wolf world, even less the Paladin one! What did that even mean?

Sage knelt beside me, looking over at me with wonder in her eyes. "Demi...was your Paladin father... an alpha?"

I swallowed hard, nodding once.

"Holy shit." Sage shook her head. "Quick, nip her wrist. I read that the Paladin alphas are old school. They bite their members to claim them and tie their soul to their people so that they can share power. I think...you could save her?" Sage sounded unsure, but definitely looked heartbroken at the sight of the innocent dying sixteen-year-old girl.

Alpha. Bite her? Tie my soul? What the hell was happening?

The girl blinked up at me, a single tear running down her cheek. "It's okay. Father will take me now."

Father as in the *heavenly* father? Hell no, I wasn't letting her die.

"Not yet," I growled, a need to save this girl surging within me.

I picked up her wrist and looked at the several thin white scars there. Old teeth marks. From my father, Run? My grandfather?

As if my body knew what to do, my teeth lengthened, pressing onto my bottom lip. I looked at Sage as if asking for direction, and she winced before shrugging. Walsh was silent behind me and I snapped into action. Taking her delicate wrist into my mouth, I clamped down until the flesh pierced, like biting into an apple.

She cried out and I pulled my mouth away, frowning when the coppery tang hit my tongue.

'*Mine,*' my wolf exclaimed inside of me.

Whatever this girl was, her name, age, all of that was unknown to me, but her essence, who she was, her soul, I knew instantly. She was soft-spoken, sweet, powerful, special, loyal as all hell, and submissive. I *knew* this.

'*Pack,*' my wolf howled inside of me.

"Pack," I said aloud, and a tug pulled at my chest as her back arched, a gasp of pain ripping from her throat. Blue glittery magic flew out from every pore in her skin, and then like a vacuum it sucked right back into her. A pressure, like a hundred-pound blanket, pressed into my

145

back and I groaned at the discomfort. Whatever was happening was happening to the both of us. The blue glitter absorbed into her every pore until her skin was once again pale and milky.

She pulled her hands away from her stomach and the gash began to knit together right before our eyes. I looked back at Sage, and now at Walsh too, who stared in wonder at the naked girl with the most amazing magic I'd ever seen.

Sage shrugged off her deer fur and laid it over the girl as she sat up and looked at me. "Thank you, Alpha." She dipped her head submissively, unable to meet my eyes.

I frowned. "Uh. You're welcome... What's your name?"

She pulled the deer fur on, tying it up the front, and then shrugged on some sweatpants that Sage tossed her from my backpack.

She looked timid at my question. "My name is Astra, my Alpha."

I cringed. "Don't...call me Alpha, okay?"

Her eyes widened in horror. "Yes, Alph—okay."

She looked confused by my behavior and I felt bad for some reason, but this was all freaking me out. I'd just bit her and my wolf claimed her and it was way too much for me to process.

"There is something you need to know, Alp..." She shook her head. "Our people—" A shout came from somewhere behind our trail and her eyes widened in fear.

146

Walsh crawled to the front, taking the reins of the horse. "Let's chat later," he said, and kicked the horse in the side, causing it to gallop away.

The girl's whole body shook in fear as the carriage jerked to a start and we moved farther and farther away from the shouting men. I could *feel* her. Like a frightened bunny about to be eaten, her entire body shook as fear pulsed through her, making her heart patter against her chest. I felt her similar to how I could feel Sawyer's moods or hear his thoughts through our imprint, Astra and I had a connection ...but different. Sisterly. Familial.

I instinctively placed an arm on her shoulder and her shaking stopped as my calmness threaded through whatever bond we had and into her. She nuzzled up against my side and I looked at Sage. My redheaded bestie was giving me a look I didn't like, one of complete and utter confusion. It made me feel alien and weird.

"Sawyer isn't responding," I told Sage, remembering in that moment my failed attempts to reach him.

Walsh whipped the reins, and the horse ran faster. "Something must be wrong," he said.

For someone who had just nearly died, he sure bounced back quickly. I looked down at the frail brown-haired girl curled around my leg, and one word reverberated through my head.

Alpha.

Alpha.

Alpha.

She'd called me Alpha and it had felt...right. I bit her. Claimed her? It wasn't as weird and sexual as it sounded. She was family and I felt like we'd finally found each other after a long time away. These new thoughts scared me, what they meant for me, Sawyer, and my place with him. My future alpha, my future husband.

CHAPTER EIGHT

WE RODE HARD AND FAST THROUGH THE DARK FEY lands until the sun was just beginning to set on the horizon. The bright orange flags marking the end of Dark Fey Territory and the beginning of Light Fey City stood out on the horizon. Not just flags, but there was a high stone wall and a few signs. Dozens of signs every three of four feet: "Dark Fey keep out," "Light Fey Only," "Turn back or lose your head."

Yikes.

Walsh pulled on the reins, slowing the wagon; the horse came to a full stop.

'Sawyer? Are you okay? We just made it to Light Fey City. Gonna grab a car and I should be at the Witch Lands in a couple hours.'

Nothing. Not even a feeling. He'd gone completely dark.

Crap.

Walsh "parked" the horse and carriage at the edge of the dark fey lands and dismounted. My gaze flicked to the girl wrapped around my leg. Astra. She was like a stage five clinger and I wasn't sure I was ready to just send her to find her way home on her own. Even in her human form she just held on to me or leaned into me and watched our surroundings with unease.

Walsh must have been thinking the same thing. He looked up at her from his place on the ground and extended his hand. "Come on. We'll see you home. You can pass through the Light Fey City with us into the Witch Lands, and then make it home through Wolf City."

She swallowed hard, looking at his outstretched hand with fear. Something dark slithered across my mind. What had men done to her to make her so fearful of them?

She looked up at me and I nodded. "You can trust him."

Without hesitation she stood and took Walsh's outstretched hand as he helped her to descend the carriage. I was next, and finally Sage. We stood, the four of us, bruised, bloody, but not broken. What a shit show these entire last few days had been, but we were almost there.

"We cross the fence and I'll find us a car," Walsh stated.

I nodded curtly, my stomach in knots over the fact that Sawyer had gone completely quiet.

We approached the fence slowly, looking left and right. I half expected a sniper to shoot us down the second we crossed over, but after swinging my legs over the brick wall and hitting the rocks, I was relieved to see my head still attached to my body.

I looked around and took in Light Fey City.

Whoa.

In direct contrast to Dark Fey Territory, black asphalt roads and shiny modern buildings with solar paneled rooftops dotted the distance. Astra huddled close to me like a little loyal chihuahua, shaking like one too. Sage caught my gaze and frowned at her, obviously worried about what had the girl so scared.

What had those motherfuckers done to her back there? Did they know she could heal people? Probably not or they'd have never let her go. I shook off my anger and we walked down the asphalt road, stopping in a thick outcrop of trees as we reached a neighborhood of track homes. Walsh glanced at a black BMW and looked over at us.

"I'll be right back. If anyone comes, kill them. We can't afford to sound the alarm that we are in enemy territory. Not here. They have modern technology and a huge army. There will be a contingent of guards on us in seconds."

Astra squeaked in fear and I nodded to Walsh. "Will do."

Considering we'd left in such a rush and sadly I left

behind the fey blade and shotgun, I didn't really have any weapons to kill anyone.

After he jogged away, I turned to poor Astra. She lowered her chin even farther as my eyes looked her over, really taking her in. She had a smattering of freckles across her face, but there were fine scars all over her body. Her neck, cheeks, chest. Little lacelike webbing of previous injuries. Previous injuries she had healed?

"Look at me," I commanded, because it was the only way she seemed to be able to respond. I felt a small measure of power leave my body and wash over her and it terrified me. Was that...alpha power? Like what Sawyer did? And his father?

Her chin jutted up to look at me with those swimming blue eyes.

"You saved Walsh. That makes you my friend and I don't let *anything* happen to my friends. Understand?"

She swallowed hard and nodded.

Sage tipped her head. "Me neither. Anyone fucks with you again, they lose their head right before I shove it up their ass." She raised a fist for good measure.

Astra's eyes bugged and I shot Sage a look that said to tone down the descriptive killing. This girl seemed very sheltered, like she'd been plucked right out of a nunnery. But our assurances and threats had worked to calm her. She stopped shaking and looked in wonder at the black sleek car that pulled out toward us, Walsh at the wheel.

Had she never seen a car?

We rushed forward, Sage taking the front and Astra and I popping into the back. I closed the door and slipped on my seatbelt as Astra looked around, wide-eyed. Her gaze tracked the ceiling, the console with all its lights, and the seatbelt at my waist.

Walsh gunned it, making the tires screech a little and I knew he was probably going to drive like a bat out of hell. Reaching over, I clipped Astra in, tucking the belt over Sage's deer fur that she wore, and the sweatpants.

"It keeps you in the car if there is an accident and we bonk into something." I was treating her like a child and I felt bad for that, but she was so naive and innocent. I just wanted to protect her.

She nodded.

'Sawyer, I'm coming. Where are you?' I growled in my head, getting more and more frustrated that he wasn't responding. If Meredith or her mother had done anything to him again, I was going to kill them both.

I didn't have time to really enjoy Light Fey City. Walsh drove fast but not fast enough to draw attention to us, just enough to get us through the territory quickly. It looked like a mini–New York City: high-rise buildings and clusters of nice houses, all with modern touches; fancy cars blasted past us as we raced to the edge of the city. My parents and Raven, Sawyer said, were all waiting for me just a few miles away. I could finally put this nightmare behind me. But mostly I just wanted to be in Sawyer's arms. It had been too long without him. I missed his touch, his smell, his kisses.

"Almost there." Walsh gunned the gas as the wrought iron gates that marked the Witch Lands rose in the distance. There were two guards at either end of the open gates. Both wore long black cloaks.

Warlocks.

'Sawyer!' I shouted, wondering if I was louder, if that would help.

"Sawyer still isn't responding. What could have happened?" I asked Sage. The need to talk to someone about this was too strong.

Sage frowned, looking back at me from her spot in the front seat. "He could have been arrested and taken to Magic City Jail. Kidnapped by vampires or light fey in retaliation for killing Locke. His—"

"Ohmygod, stop." I covered my ears, rushing the words together. "I didn't *actually* want to know all the bad things that could have happened."

Sage winced. "Sorry." She reached back and clasped my hand. "Hey, I'm worried too, but my cousin has been training with Eugene for decades. No one is going to get the drop on him."

But they did. They had to have, unless this was another magic spell thing put over our bond so that we couldn't communicate.

My eyes widened. "Stop the car!" I yelled to Walsh, and the tires skidded to a halt, a black plume of smoke coming up behind us. We were twenty feet from the gate, and the two warlocks' hooded heads turned our way.

It's a trap...

It had to be. Only a witch would be able to keep Sawyer and I from speaking, like the magic in Troll Village.

Had the witches turned against us too?

"Go right, drive away from the gate. Now," I told Walsh as the two warlocks raised a gnarled wooden staff, each with a crystal ball on top.

Walsh did as I asked, and when we were a few blocks away, I released a shaky breath.

"What's up?" Walsh's gaze flicked to mine in the mirror.

"I...think maybe the witches are against us too. Or some of them at least. My bond with Sawyer is being blocked."

Probably in part because I'd torn it to pieces after he chose Meredith. *Oops.*

Walsh frowned. "You think everyone is against us now?"

Now I felt stupid and paranoid. "I don't know... Can we cut through the Wild Lands now? We're so close."

The Witch Lands and Werewolf City touched, so if we drove to the edge of the Wild Lands it would be a short trek through to the very edge of Wolf City.

"I dunno, Sage and I had a lot of Ithaki gunning for us—"

"Yes. I will get you safely across," Astra spoke from the back seat.

Walsh and Sage shared a look. "The Ithaki—"

"I'll get you safely across," she pressed, and it was the sternest I'd ever heard her.

"If she says she can, she can," I told them.

Astra and I were connected, and I could feel her genuineness. She wouldn't lead us astray. Walsh took a side road that ran the length of the wrought iron gate and headed for the Wild Lands. We passed a few openings with warlocks positioned at the entrance about every mile or so. It was the most guarded territory of them all; they really didn't want anyone going in...or out. After an hour and nearly running out of gas, we reached the back fence of Light Fey City, and there was only one sign.

Wild Lands. Enter at your own risk.

Walsh slowed the car to a crawl before pulling over and putting it into park. We all unclipped our belts and stepped out of the car, slinging backpacks over our shoulders and preparing for the final stretch back to Wolf City.

Walsh stepped toward a gap in the Wild Lands gate, but Astra clicked her tongue. "That's Ithaki land. This way." She walked along the rough, piled stone, vines creeping over the top.

Walsh frowned. "How can you tell?"

She gave him a timid look. "How can you tell where the kitchen is in your house?"

"Touché," he said.

This was her land, her home, and I had no doubt she knew every inch of it. There was a gap in the wall ahead and she headed toward it, slipping inside and disappearing behind the high stone.

Sage and Walsh looked at me as if asking one more time if I trusted her. She'd saved Walsh's life at the risk of her own. Were they losing their minds?

I stepped ahead of them and slipped in behind her, walking into a thick forest.

Astra stood quietly, waiting for us. Her entire demeanor had changed. She was relaxed, a little more confident in her own land, leaning casually against the base of a giant apple tree. Apples hung from the branches and she plucked one off, taking a bite. "Last batch of the season. They'll all be rotten or frozen in a month."

She started to skip her way down a path, and I shared a look with Sage and Walsh. My, my, how being on her own turf had changed her.

'Demi! Dammit, woman—'

Sawyer screamed inside my head and I stopped, sagging in relief at his voice. *'I'm here!'*

'Don't go into the Witch Lands! It's a trap,' he rushed out.

Everyone else stopped and looked at me. I tapped my head once and Sage relayed to them what that meant. *'I didn't. I figured it out when you didn't respond.'*

'*Where are you? I'm going unhinged. Are you okay?*' Concern threaded through his voice.

Relief washed through me now that our bond had been restored. Must have been because we were in the Wild Lands, a place the witches couldn't blanket with spell power?

'*Walsh nearly died, a healer Paladin saved his life and is now walking us from Light Fey City through Paladin Wild Lands to Werewolf City.*'

He was silent a moment. '*A Paladin helped Walsh? Are you sure you can trust them? They could be leading you into a trap.*'

'*I'm sure, Sawyer...*' I growled a little, annoyed that everyone thought the Paladins were bad when all I'd ever seen was goodness from them. '*She nearly died trying to heal him, and she's as timid as a mouse. She's barely sixteen years old!*'

'*Okay. I'm sorry, I just...I haven't slept well in days. I need you home, I need you in my bed.*' His voice was gruff, and my heart swelled.

'*I miss you too, you big idiot. Who puts on a necklace from their jealous ex-girlfriend?*'

I expected him to laugh, that maybe we were at that stage, but he didn't. '*I'll never stop trying to make that up to you, and for the record, I don't remember putting it on. Those five minutes are all black.*'

Probably a spell. Fuckers.

'*Where exactly are you?*' Sawyer asked. '*I'm coming.*

I'm bringing an army with me. This will never happen again, you will never be taken from me.' His voice held deadly promise, and I knew without a doubt if anyone tried again, they would meet their death.

'*Can you go to the southeast-most corner of Wolf City? We should come out somewhere around there,'* I guessed based on where we were walking and the map Marmal had given me.

I longed to get word to my troll friend that I had made it home safely.

'*I'll be there! We were able to magic the ankle monitor to allow me to go around Wolf City before the witches turned on us, but I cannot cross the border. I'll see you soon. Be safe,'* Sawyer said, and then I felt him retreat into my thoughts.

"Let's go. Sawyer will be waiting at the Wolf City flag line," I told everyone.

With every step deeper into Paladin land that I took, I felt something inside of me stirring. My wolf? My soul? Something felt right here, at home here. I shook it off and ran faster to catch up with Astra's skipping.

We'd been briskly walking for a good thirty minutes when I heard the snap of a twig. We all froze and turned to the sound. I felt my wolf stir just under my skin as one of the male Ithaki who had helped kidnap me from the base of Waterfall Mountain stepped out of the woods with a handful of others.

He grinned. "Hello, little demon."

I balled my hands into fists and Astra ran to my side. "You can't kill them unless they step foot on our land. And they can't kill us unless we go on theirs. It's in the peace treaty," she whispered.

I looked to the ground, trying to see if there was an indication of land markings that I may have missed. Is that what had happened when I'd fallen? I'd fallen into Ithaki land and that sweet man, my grandfather, had crossed over the line to help me?

Guilt gnawed at my chest as I realized that he'd been killed because of me. One hundred percent, I saw it then. Small blue crushed stones made a line in the damp earth, demarcating a path.

"Run along before I drag you over this line and smash your brains out," I growled to the man who had once plotted to skin me alive with that vampire-fey Eugene thankfully had shot dead.

He sneered, stepping closer to the line so that his toe was barely touching it. "You will be mine, little demon. Especially now that there is a bounty."

I swallowed hard at the word *bounty*. I'd totally forgotten about the two-million vampire bounty. I should kill him and his men right here. Who would care? I didn't give a shit about some little crushed rock line. I wanted him in pieces for what he'd done to me.

'*Alpha*,' Astra whispered, and it took me a moment to realize she had spoken in my head...like Sawyer did. Like Sage did in wolf form. Like *pack*.

I looked at her, blinking back shock.

"We *cannot* break the treaty. We can't handle a war right now," she muttered aloud this time.

I relaxed my fists, my wolf calming inside of me, taking her advice. It wouldn't be right to leave trouble on her doorstep and then go back to Wolf City. With a final glare, I began to walk forward, to an opening in the distance. All the while I felt my wolf rustle inside of me, wanting to break free and rip that Ithaki man's head off.

"Just up ahead!" Astra broke into a run, seemingly unperturbed about the Ithaki watching us leave. The treaty must be a well-respected thing. That, or she didn't want to mess with Sage and Walsh and I together. We were covered in blood and must look slightly badass. Astra skipped and twirled like a little carefree girl who was just meandering through her backyard.

The second I saw the line of orange flags, I also heard him.

Sawyer.

"Demi!" he roared into the trees.

My heart swelled in my chest as I pumped my legs, blasting past Sage and Walsh and then Astra.

"Sawyer!" Tears filled my eyes.

He chose me, he did, before we were both tricked into some horrible public break-up that wasn't even real. It felt real. Well, it was real, but it was magic, we were both tricked. A large part of me still hurt from what he'd said, but I had to remember he was under a spell.

You're just like your mother.

That wasn't magically put in his mind, was it? I just wanted to push it all under the rug and be in his arms. It's all I cared about right now. Remembering that he was wearing an ankle bracelet and couldn't come to me without getting electrocuted, I leapt as fast as possible through the final stretch of woods.

"Demi!" he shouted again, voice hoarse and frantic. I cleared the row of orange flags and broke out into a flat green grassy area. Sawyer was to the right, looking into the woods, and over fifty armed men sprawled out into the green park behind him.

"I'm here!" I yelled, and he spun.

When my eyes fell on him, my heart sank. Dark circles hung under his eyes; he hadn't shaved in days, and a black, bulky leg cuff marred his ankle. When he saw me, he sagged with relief and staggered backward. His hungry gaze ran the length of my body as if looking for wounds, or marks, or some sign of what I'd been through. And he found many. His gaze stopped over each bruise, each patch of blood until his eyes narrowed to slits.

I ran and his arms opened as I leapt into them, feeling them tighten around me. His earthy, musky scent enveloped me and I whimpered.

"Thank fuck," he rasped against my neck, breathing me in. "I nearly burned the whole world down looking for you."

He held me as silent tears slipped down my face. I'd never loved someone this much, loved them so much that it physically hurt. I was back in his arms, and yet I couldn't get the painful sting of his voice out of my head.

I choose Meredith Pepper to be my wife.

I wondered then about what Raven had told me, about love potions only being able to amplify already existing feelings. I pulled back from him and gave him a tight smile as he reached out and brushed a tear away from my cheek.

"Happy tears or sad ones?" He frowned, his muscles tightening as if anticipating a hit.

I swallowed hard. "Both."

His frown deepened, making his chin butt pucker, and I reached out and stroked it. "You chose Meredith. In front of everyone..." My voice cracked.

He whimpered like a dog that had just been run over by a car; it was pained and loud. "No!" He fell to his knees, hugging my waist and nuzzling his face into my stomach. "Fuck no. That was magic. I choose you. Always. Forever. Please..." His voice broke. "Forgive me."

I looked down at him, and he looked up at me and I grinned. "You on your knees is kind of a nice look."

A slow smirk played across his face. "Oh baby, I can do a lot on my knees." He flicked his eyes to between my legs and my entire body warmed.

It wasn't lost on me that the future alpha of all of

Werewolf City was on his knees in the dirt and grass, hugging my waist and begging for forgiveness in front of his entire alpha army, who snuck side glances at the spectacle.

"I won't get up until you forgive me. No matter how emasculating it is." He stayed on his knees, looking up at me like a lost puppy.

I grinned. "Maybe just one more minute."

He growled, playfully, and grabbed me by the legs in excitement as he shot up to his feet. I squealed as he carried me over his shoulder in a fireman pose before sliding me down his chest, rubbing my breasts all the way down his body and causing his eyes to turn the color of molten lava.

"Future Mrs. Hudson," he breathed in the sexiest voice I'd ever heard, "will you please forgive me for getting spelled with an evil necklace and being mind-controlled by my ex-girlfriend?"

When he put it that way, it wasn't really his fault, was it?

"Future Mrs. Calloway-Hudson actually. I'm hyphenating and you haven't *technically* asked me to marry you yet."

His eyes glittered. "No. I haven't *yet.*"

He slipped his hand into mine and then turned to face Walsh and Sage and Astra, who stepped out of the woods.

All fifty guards raised their guns at the sight of Astra

and I thrust my hands out. "No! She's with us!" I ripped my hand from Sawyer's and ran over to her side. She was shaking like a leaf again, eyes on the ground. Sawyer's men lowered their guns and looked to him.

"You're okay. They won't hurt you," I told her, placing a protective hand on her shoulder.

She looked back at the woods. "Need to get home."

I nodded, about to ask if she needed help getting back, when Sawyer stepped up behind me, extending his hand to her. "I heard about what you did for my best friend, and I just wanted to thank you for healing him."

This was big. Super big. To have the future Werewolf City alpha offering to shake hands with a Paladin wolf. She must have known it too, because she looked at me and I gave her a curt nod. Then she stuck out her hand and shook his.

"Is there anything I can offer you in form of payment? Gold or—?"

She hissed, "Blasphemy."

Sawyer looked at me and I shrugged, as if to say I had no idea what she was rattling on about. She seemed super religious or spiritual or whatever.

"All right, well. Thanks again." Sawyer let go of her hand and slipped an arm around my shoulders. Astra looked between us and then at the woods.

"Alpha?" Astra said timidly, and I flinched.

Sawyer seemed to think she was talking to him. "My father is actually, but I'm next in line."

Lord help me...

This was *not* a conversation I wanted to have with him right now.

The entire idea that I could be a Paladin alpha... the *last* Paladin alpha by my count, drove my thoughts to wild places. I looked over at her and her eyes were glistening with tears. "Aren't you coming home? With me?" she asked me.

Home. What a funny word. I'd never felt like I had a home, growing up banished in the human world with the rest of the magical rejects.

Sawyer stiffened against me and I swallowed hard.

"This is my home." The lie flew from my mouth with ease, tasting like ashes on my tongue. "Wherever Sawyer is...is my home." That rang true and felt better in my mouth. Wolf City was still a stranger's land to me, but Sawyer was where I wanted to be.

She frowned. *'But our people—'*

"Goodbye, Astra. I'm glad you're safe now," I told her. I needed her to go before I lost my shit. I felt the strongest urge to rip my clothes from my body, shift into my wolf and run across the flag line and into the Paladin lands howling at the moon as I went. My wolf and I felt more like one being on those lands, and that scared me.

She looked unsure. Scared. Sick. Her wide eyes registered me with shock.

'You're staying here?' Her voice in my head was full of hurt, and I swallowed hard and nodded.

"Do you need to be escorted back to your village?" Sawyer asked kindly, misinterpreting the fear in her eyes.

She shook her head, wiping away a lone tear. "No." She started to walk away, but when she reached the flag line, she looked back at me, and I was such a coward I couldn't meet her gaze.

My heart fluttered against my rib cage as she stared at me.

'Paladin people are blessed. Without an alpha to anchor us, our magic withers and dies. You must come home. Soon.' Her words in my head sent shivers down my spine.

Home.

Home.

Home.

"That was weird," Sawyer commented, snapping me out of my stupor.

I reached for him, and he for me.

"Tell me everything," he said, brushing a piece of hair from my cheek.

I nodded. "Are my parents safe? Raven?"

"Yes. I got them out of the Witch Lands before things got scary there."

I didn't even want to know what "got scary there" meant.

Marmal flew into my mind and I squeezed his arm. "I need to get a message to someone first, then we can talk."

After handwriting a lengthy note and inquiring as to the well-being of Ginny, I gave the note to one of Sawyer's guards and he agreed to get it to Marmal of Rosedale.

Walsh and Sage both agreed to catch up with us later. Sawyer and I went to his apartment, where he ordered tons of food and I told him everything about my trip. Almost everything. I left out Arrow and the alpha stuff. I hadn't even really processed that information myself, and I didn't think it was going to do any good right now with Sawyer having his own problems to worry about.

"Now your turn," I told him.

He scrubbed his face before popping a strawberry into his mouth and looking at me across the dinner table next to his kitchen. "I need you to know that I wasn't myself when I found you kissing that fake motherfucker who I will most certainly find and kill."

I swallowed hard but didn't say anything as he continued. "It was like I was possessed. Possessed with rage and hatred for you, and drunk on fake love and adoration for Meredith. But also confused because I still loved you. It's like they couldn't take that from me."

Pain sliced through my chest, making my entire body ache as I remembered the moment he cast me out of my own engagement party and declared Meredith his future wife.

"Raven told me once that you can't make a love spell work on someone you don't have feelings for..."

There, I said it.

He nodded as he ran his fingers through his hair. "Look, Meredith and I were together for two years. I *did* love her at the time, but she changed. Became colder and calculating, more controlling. I do *not* love her anymore, but I still cared about what happened to her. It's why I pulled her aside to tell her I was going to pick you. I cared that she wasn't hurt publicly, and I think that care for her well-being was what fueled the spell."

I snorted. "Ironic considering you publicly humiliated me."

Pain and shame crossed his features, making his face contort into a grimace. "I'm a *complete* fucking asshole for that. Magic aside. I remember everything I said and did. It was like watching a train wreck and I couldn't stop it." He stood, walked over to my chair, and bent down in front of me. "I've messed up a lot with you, haven't I?"

My mind went to the time he forcibly cuffed me, and then with Meredith, and I nodded. But I knew everything he did was because he thought he was protecting me. Or he was magically drugged by his ex.

"Allow me *one more* chance." He reached out and grabbed my hips, pulling me onto his lap. "One more chance and I'll get it right. I promise I won't fuck up this time."

His blue eyes searched mine desperately, and I couldn't help the warmth that thawed my heart. People made mistakes, but a man that could admit them, apologize, and try to do better, was worth his weight in gold.

"There is a way you could make it up to me." My voice dropped into deep sexy bedroom talk and his eyes went half lidded.

"Oh, Miss Calloway, please do tell."

I grinned, pulling at the edges of my shirt and tugging it over my head, careful to still baby my shoulder. "I need a shower."

His breath came out in a rush as he wet his lips with his tongue. Then his gaze fell on my shoulder and his arms stiffened around me. "You're hurt. Who did that?" he growled.

I knew that if I hadn't already killed the troll, that Sawyer would go on another murder spree in my honor.

"A dead man. Focus. Shower?"

With a growl, he stood, clutching me to his chest as his warm breath washed over my face.

"You placed smiles like flowers on the altar of my heart." He peppered my neck with kisses as I threaded my fingers through his hair.

"Who?" I panted, wanting to know the poet and forgetting about Sawyer's penchant for reciting sweet nothings to me.

"John O'Donohue." He kissed me tenderly as we stepped into the bathroom. He set my feet down on the floor and I slowly stripped, peeling off my dirty travel clothes. I backed up against the wall so he could pass by me and turn on the hot water. When he spun back around to face me, he looked at my body and his jaw clenched so tightly that I thought his teeth might snap. I looked down, unsure what upset him, and saw that I was riddled with bruises and small cuts.

He reached up and cupped my face. "Not being there, not being able to find you myself..." He leaned his forehead against mine. "...it *killed* me." He rubbed at the stubble on his face and I couldn't help but remark at how lucky I was to be loved by him. Reaching for his shirt, he pulled it off in one quick move and I noticed that he too had his own fading bruises. A fading bruise on a werewolf meant it had to be a really bad wound or broken bone. Probably from his fight with Locke. My eyes fell to the ankle monitor at his leg and I shook my head, stepping closer to him.

"You shouldn't have done that. With Vicon Drake. Now you're on trial for murder and—"

"And it was worth it. Every fucking second of his murder was worth it no matter the consequence, you understand me?" His voice was like sandpaper and I gulped, nodding. Sawyer stepped into the shower and then reached a hand out for me, pulling me inside with him.

The warm water that hit my skin was heaven, trailing down my back and washing all the dirt and blood off of me. Sawyer watched me, pumping some liquid soap onto his hands, making suds before running them over my arms and then my breasts. He lathered my body with suds, trailing his fingers over my nipples, which tightened to points, leaving a searing trail of heat in their wake. I panted, grabbing some soap and doing the same to him. When his lips fell onto mine, I parted them eagerly, meeting his tongue in the middle.

My fingers ran over his chest, raking down his abs. I'd forgotten how tight his muscles were. Massaging him was like trying to massage a rock. His slick and soapy hand trailed down my navel and my thighs, clenched with need. When one of his fingers slipped inside of me, I let out a deep, satisfying groan. Our bond opened then, and all of the fragmented bits started to mend together again. I could feel his possessive and all-consuming love for me, his shame and regret over the incident with Meredith, and his pure hatred for her now. He massaged between my legs as I panted and reached for him, my tongue sliding against his. Wrapping my hands around his hardness, I began to stroke him as he huffed against my mouth. Water rolled down our faces as we pleasured each other and I felt our imprint spark stronger with each throaty kiss.

"Confession," Sawyer huffed, deep and husky in my ear.

"What?" I gasped, barely able to concentrate as he wound his fingers rapidly on the most sensitive part of me.

He pulled back and his fiery blue gaze held mine.

"I'm terrified you'll be my undoing. Because I'll never deny you anything. I'm at your mercy, Demi Calloway. Be aware of the power you hold over me."

I shattered into a million pieces then, a climax racking my body as his words sank into my heart and seeped throughout my soul.

CHAPTER NINE

S AWYER AND I FELL ASLEEP PRETZELED IN EACH other's arms, limbs intertwined, breathing steadily in sync. It was like no time had passed. The only thing amiss was that I'd dreamed of Astra—her sweet innocent face looking at me in shock.

'Alpha? Aren't you coming home?'

I tossed and turned all night, her words echoing in my head until I woke up damp with sweat.

"Would you like to take the semester off?" Sawyer asked, pulling me from my thoughts as he stepped out of the shower, steam filtering out through his back.

I shook my head. "No. I'm ready to go back."

There was a knock on the door, and he wrapped the towel around his waist as water dripped down the V marks on his abs.

Good lord, this man was yummy.

I popped into the bathroom to brush my teeth, and when I came out there was a tray of breakfast on the bed. A single pink rose sat in a vase, and there was a white scroll tied to the rose with ribbon.

I looked up at him and he looked nervous. "Letter for you."

I grinned, imagining him writing it while I was brushing my teeth. My heart pounded in my chest as I scanned the food for a wedding ring. He still hadn't asked me. Would he do it like this? Intimate and low key?

My stomach flipped over with nerves as I peeled off the paper and read the note.

Move in with me? Yes or No.

A little pencil rolled out and there was a square check box for me to write my answer. A grin pulled at my lips.

I pretended to think, tapping my chin and he growled, which just caused me to grin wider.

"Woman," he snarled, as laughter pealed out of me.

I checked *yes* and handed it back to him. He glanced down at the paper and sighed in obvious relief. "Oh good, because I already have Roland packing your things from your old dorm."

I reached out and smacked his chest. "Confident much?"

His smile fell. "With you? Not really. I can't even believe you're still with me after all this."

I stroked his cheek. "I mean you were love spelled. I have to give you some credit there." I grabbed a bagel and started to spread the cream cheese.

"Finish breakfast quickly. I have a surprise for you." Leaning over, he kissed my cheek and started to tap away on his tablet.

Hated surprises, but I nodded. Moving in with Sawyer?

No. Big. Deal.

I gulped. This was next-level relationship stuff. I would miss Lexington Hall and seeing Sage all the time. Hopefully, she would still come over. I was too young to be part of some old married couple already who never went out.

After finishing breakfast, I changed into clothes that Sawyer had brought over for me and followed him outside. Sage and Walsh were leaning against the door of his apartment wearing their alpha security guard uniforms. Walsh and Sawyer bro hugged, and Sage slid next to me. "Did you say yes? To moving in?" She grinned as we all started to walk.

I nodded, causing her to smile. "But you better come over all the time."

She pulled a silver key out of her pocket. "I have a key. I'll be all up in your business."

"Hey, that's for emergencies," Sawyer spoke over his shoulder to his cousin.

Sage nodded, saluting him. "Like when I have an emergency and can't curl the back of my hair myself."

We erupted into laugher and she slung her arm into mine. It was crazy to think that just a few days ago I was fighting for my life, broken, depressed, and now everything was back to normal. I kept waiting for the other shoe to drop; it didn't seem real. My gaze flicked to the black ankle bracelet on Sawyer's leg and reality came crashing down. When would that shitstorm come calling?

Hopefully never, but I just didn't think so.

We crossed through the main outdoor space, and I noticed that students were looking at Sawyer differently. With more respect, pride. Their future alpha's ankle bracelet and kill record had clearly started a reputation. Off in the distance, dozens of guards roamed the perimeter, and Eugene stalked behind us a good twenty paces, hobbling on a cane. I was glad to see he'd made it and was doing okay. Wolf City seemed ready for an attack at any time...

Because of me? I didn't want to ask that question.

When we reached the parking lot, Sawyer pushed a button on a key fob and a white Range Rover beeped, flashing its lights. Then he handed the fob to me casually. "Okay, I had this outfitted with bulletproof glass, fire shield, and biohazard air filters. If you get in a scary situation, you can literally just wait it out in the car until I can reach you and you'll survive." He pulled out his phone. "I have a GPS tracker on it and—"

I sputtered, holding my hands out. "Wait, what?"

He frowned, looking at me. "This is your car. I bought it for you."

I swallowed hard. Bulletproof glass? Biohazard air filters? Were we expecting an anthrax attack or something?

"Sawyer...I don't even have a driver's license."

His eyes widened. "Oh." He looked to Walsh. "Can you set her up with private lessons with Eugene? Include that kidnapper course they made my mom take after I was taken."

Kidnapper driving course. My eyebrows hit my hairline. He noticed the distress in my face and pulled me aside. "We'll meet you in the car," he told Walsh and Sage.

They nodded, walking away, and Sawyer wrapped me into his arms, hugging me, and then pulled back to look at me. "I know you didn't really know what you were signing up for when you started dating me, but this is it. Bulletproof glass and special evasive driving techniques. It's all necessary when you're the alpha's wife. Even more so when you're a split shifter that everyone wants in their possession." His last words were a growl.

I swallowed hard. *Alpha's wife.* Even though he still hadn't technically asked me. Maybe he wouldn't? Maybe it was just assumed? I shook my head. "No, it's fine. I'm just...overwhelmed."

He reached out with a warm hand and stroked my cheek with his knuckles. "We'll get through it together." He then plastered on a mischievous grin. "Now can we get to the surprise? I'm dying to show you."

The car wasn't the surprise? Nerves churned in my gut. Was he finally going to propose? Properly?

"Come on." He yanked me forward, grinning like a fool. Whatever it was had him excited, and so I was going to be excited too. Jogging after him, I pulled at my T-shirt that read *Sorry I'm late, I didn't want to come.* Maybe this was a bad choice for a possible proposal outfit? Why did I suck so bad at this? Meredith would have worn a minidress every day of the week until Sawyer proposed. I just didn't have the energy or desire.

We got into the car and Sawyer sped off down the road. I stared at the black leather, the fancy silver knobs, and inhaled the brand-new smell. He bought me a car. A *brand-new* car that could survive a zombie apocalypse. My gaze flicked to the rearview mirror to see Walsh and Sage right behind us.

"Any hints on my surprise?" I asked.

Sawyer grinned but said nothing. We left campus and turned away from downtown, heading for the suburbs.

I watched contentedly as the trees and buildings passed by, while Sawyer's thumb stroked small circles on my thigh. It was weird to have been through everything and now jump right back into life like nothing happened. I looked at Sawyer and I could see the cool, calm, collectedness he always carried. It's like we hadn't both just nearly died and people weren't chasing after me to "consume my essence." As long as we were together, he seemed okay, and I was too. Just glad to be back in his arms.

"Is there something you want to talk about?" He looked over at me and I realized I was staring at him.

I swallowed. "It was just a rough few days. Feels surreal to be back and...I dunno, doing normal stuff."

His lips pulled into a frown and he nodded. "Do you need to talk to someone about it? I mean, see someone? No shame—"

"No." I waved him off. "Just...venting."

His hand squeezed my thigh. "You can talk to me if you want. I mean, I know you told me the basics of what happened, but..." He trailed off.

I nodded, glad that he wasn't a guy who was afraid of emotional depth. "The troll girl who helped me?" I said.

He nodded, pulling off the highway and onto a large street lined with trees.

"Her name was Marmal and she was a badass. She was...attacked by the vampires at a young age and her neighbor taught her to shoot a shotgun. So now she runs a farm by herself and the vampires don't fuck with her."

Sawyer grinned. "I like her already."

I smiled. "And I want a shotgun now! And did you know the dark fey have high priestesses that can shoot black magic nets out of their mouths?"

He growled; it was more of a painful whine, and I quieted.

"I did," he said. "And it kills me to not have been there with you, helping get you out of it." His eyes flicked jealously to the rearview mirror for a millisecond.

I pointed to the ankle bracelet on his leg. "You couldn't. I understand."

His hand tightened on the steering wheel. "I'm going to make sure you're never taken from me again."

I reached out and stroked his hair as he turned into a nice community of what looked like brand-new houses. "That's sweet, but I'm not sure it's possible."

He chuckled, dark and dry. "Fucking let them try again." His voice could cut glass, and I knew better than to keep pushing it. His wolf was too close to the surface, and he wouldn't see reason.

"We need to find out more about what I am and what I can do, why exactly people are after me," I told him.

Every single muscle in his body clenched. "Power, Demi. They are after you for power. Fully trained, you are the strongest of all of them. They want that, they want to be drunk on that, so much so that they threw away a centuries-old peace accord in an effort to get a taste."

Chills ran up my spine. "So the witches turned on us too?"

He nodded. "Most of them. They are breaking in two as we speak, just like the fey did so long ago. Some may side with us, but it doesn't look good."

I gulped. "If everyone is against us, how will we fight off an attack on our own?"

He sighed. "You let me worry about that, love. I want you to focus on today and this surprise I have for you."

I took the hint. No one wanted a downer at a party or wherever we were going. I would table this talk. For now.

When we pulled up to a beautiful two-story home, I noticed a black matching Range Rover to mine sitting in the driveway. It looked brand-new. The home was modern, white with black trim and luscious landscaping. The driveway was cobblestone. This wasn't your entry level neighborhood, it was deluxe.

Did he buy us a house?

Already? Away from town? Was that his car?

My mind spun as he stepped out of the car and opened my door, taking my hand in his. We stepped out onto the curb and he gave Sage and Walsh a nod as we passed. They remained in their car.

"Did I mention I hate surprises?" I told him as we stepped up to the walking path and through a cute garden trellis before standing at a black front door.

"You did." He grinned and knocked twice.

Okay, if he's knocking, it means he doesn't have a key...so this probably isn't our future hou—

All of the breath whooshed from my lungs when the door peeled back to reveal my mother.

"Demi!" Her voice held worry and relief as we crashed into each other at the same time. My mother wasn't big on emotion usually. This time was different. I felt her body rack with a sob as we held on to each other tightly.

"We were so worried," her muffled voice came into my shoulder.

I nodded. "I'm okay."

Sawyer stood there patiently as we held each other, until we finally pulled back, wiping at our eyes. There was something softer about my mom since she'd revealed her big Paladin secret to me. Maybe the reason she was cold and full of rough edges was because she was harboring that secret this entire time.

"Hey, kiddo!" My dad's voice came from deeper down the hall and I stepped into the house to greet him. He picked me up and spun me around while I laughed wildly. This was the best surprise ever.

It hit me then that I hadn't introduced Sawyer to my parents yet!

When he set me down, I turned to Sawyer, who still stood in the doorway. I'd just ran into some random person's house to hug my parents and poor Sawyer was waiting for an invite.

"Sorry, you guys, this is Sawyer," I told my parents.

My dad stepped forward and shook his hand. "Of course. Good to see you again. Come on in, son."

Son? Come on in? My dad said that like it was...

My mouth popped open as tears lined my eyes. "Wait...Is this your...?"

Sawyer placed an arm around my shoulders. "Your parents are now Werewolf City citizens again. This is their house, and you can see them anytime you like."

I fucking ugly cried then. Like full-on, Kim Kardashian contorted-face ugly cry. He got his dad to agree to letting my mom come back? He bought them a house? It was too much.

My mom and dad slipped out of the room to give us privacy and Sawyer pulled me into his chest, probably so he didn't have to see my ugly, crying face.

"You did this?" I sobbed into his shoulder. "Why are you so perfect? Stop it. You're making me look bad." I sniffled.

He pulled me back and wiped the tears off my cheeks. "I told you, Wolf Girl, I intend to spend the rest of my life making things up to you."

Swoon.

"So your dad just...let my parents come back?" I pressed him.

Sawyer shrugged. "He's deferring to me since I'm in training to take over next year. He's a stubborn man and won't admit wrongdoing, but I know he feels bad about what he did to your mother, banishing her like that. I overheard him talking to my mom about it recently."

He'd freaking better feel bad. I mean, seeing the woman you loved sleeping with your sworn enemy wasn't ideal, but to banish her from the pack for life to live in the human world? Too harsh.

"And this house? I mean...how will they pay for—?"

"I bought it for them with part of my inheritance."

He smiled softly like it was no big deal. "I mean, it's the least I can do for my future in-laws."

My throat clogged with emotion. "Future in-laws? Are we engaged?" I asked finally. I was fully confused.

He winked. "Not yet. I haven't asked you, remember?"

Bastard. So he was planning something...the very thought had excitement rolling through me. Pulling me down the hall, he led me into the kitchen, where the smell of my mother's white chicken enchiladas hit my nose.

Yum.

The kitchen was amazing. White cabinets with white marble that had thin gray lines running across the length of a giant island, where my dad sat on a barstool eating chips and salsa. He watched my mom bend over and pull something out of the oven, totally checking out her ass.

"Hubba-hubba," he murmured, and my mom burst into laughter, smacking him with a towel.

I grinned. After all these years they were still smitten with each other.

This was nicer than any home they'd ever known. And I knew my father, he was a proud man. There was no way he'd just taken this gift from Sawyer without a fight.

"This place is...amazing," I said. "I'm so glad you guys will be close by."

My dad nodded. "Well, it's your house, kiddo. We are just renting it from you. Right, Sawyer?" My father looked at Sawyer, who cleared his throat nervously.

"Yes, sir. I bought it for you, Demi, after your father made it clear he wouldn't take it."

Ahh, that made more sense. And wow. A house and a car today...

"So, Demi..." Sawyer popped a chip into his mouth. "Congrats, you're actually your parents' landlord."

A huge grin swept across my face. My father would never take such a generous gift for himself, but if Sawyer put the house in my name, he wouldn't deny anything for his only daughter. It was smart, and I obviously would never sell it, letting them live here forever only a ten-minute drive away from me.

"Oh, I could have some fun with that," I told them.

My dad grinned. "The neighbors are doctors and lawyers. What do you think they will think of me mowing my own lawn?" my dad asked in his usual joking manner.

I chortled. "Be sure to wear those ratty grass-stained jeans you have."

Everyone laughed, and we all slipped into an easy banter.

My dad was a jokester, and Sawyer was quickly keying into their personalities. After we sat down to eat, Sawyer took one bite of the enchiladas and groaned. "Holy smokes, these are amazing."

My mom smiled. "Thank you, Sawyer, and thank you for putting a good word in at Werewolf Elementary. I'm going to love teaching third grade."

My father nodded. "And thanks for getting me the construction job."

"You're very welcome," Sawyer told them, cheeks going pink.

He got them jobs too!

My ovaries nearly exploded.

Wow, I was only gone three or four days. My man had been busy.

'Sawyer...that was incredibly sweet,' I sent through our bond.

He smiled over at me. *'I tried to tell them they didn't need to work. I could set them up with a monthly stipend, but they weren't having it.'*

No way. My parents were hardworking people. My dad couldn't sit still. It was a miracle he was still sitting for dinner and not trying to clean up the mess my mom made while cooking.

'They'll be happier this way,' I told him.

He nodded, and then looked at my father, who had just stood to collect plates. "I'll help you clean up, sir. Then I wanted to show you the control panel in the garage for the solar panel system."

My father nodded and started to stack plates on his arm as Sawyer got our glasses.

"Come on, I want to show you the pool." My mom

187

stood and rubbed her belly. For as long as I could remember it had been this way. Mom cooked, Dad cleaned. I was raised in an equal household, and I was happy to see doing a dish or two wouldn't kill Sawyer. He'd probably never done dishes in his life.

I linked arms with my mom as she pulled me through the hallway.

"Is Raven safe?" I asked suddenly. I hadn't gotten around to getting a new phone, but I wanted to check in with her.

My mom nodded. "She's safer at Delphi. The witches are having their own civil war right now, so Sawyer had her taken back to Spokane where she can lay low."

I sighed. Poor Raven. What must it have been like for her to be in the Witch Lands finally and be waiting for me with my mom, when she was pulled back out again?

My mom opened the large glass double doors and my mouth popped open at the lush backyard. It wasn't huge, but it was a well-done space. To the right were empty cedar beds for gardening, and to the left was a stunning rectangular swimming pool. In the center was a small, trimmed strip of grass with various trees and bushes all around it.

"Honey, Sawyer told us what you are..." my mother whispered, catching me off guard. "A split shifter."

I froze, unable to say anything, and she carried on.

"I mean, he had to. I threatened to kill him multiple times." She laughed nervously.

Wow, I would have paid to see that. I wished I had been the one to tell them, but I understood that with my disappearance they would have been asking a lot of questions, namely why the heck the vampires wanted me in the first place.

"That's a good man there." My mom gestured to the house. "He was so patient with your father and me and he fought *so hard* looking for you."

My throat squeezed. "He's pretty perfect...now if only he would *actually* propose to me..."

My mom grinned. "Oh, honey, I'm not even sure this house has solar panels."

I frowned, taken off guard by her random comment about the house after I'd just confessed I was waiting to be proposed to. "Wait, what?"

My mom spun me around and tipped my chin up to the roof, sans solar panels. "I don't think Sawyer wants to take your dad into the garage to talk about solar panels."

Oh.

Ohhhh.

A huge grin swept across my face. "You think...he's asking dad for permission?"

She nodded.

I did a totally lame involuntary squeal and my mom laughed, looking younger and less worn-out than she did in the human world. Coming back to Werewolf City had brightened her. The bad days were behind her and my father. All because of Sawyer.

"Honey, back to the split-shifter thing..." My mom smoothed the top of my hair and forced me to face her. I was hoping she didn't want to get into it; it would probably turn into a big crying fest. I mean, my soul split in half because I was raped; it wasn't a pretty topic.

"Only Paladins can transform into split shifters. Run grew up with one. A woman who was trapped in a house fire. Her wolf split and dragged her human out half-dead. He talked about her to me often."

Oh lord. Chills ran up my arms at the news that there might be another like me. "You think she's still there? With the Paladins?"

My mom shrugged. "I mean, I don't see why not. She would be a bit older than me by now. Anyway, I just wanted you to know...in case you needed to find someone else to talk to."

Something brightened in my chest. If this other split shifter had lived this entire time without the vampires or anyone coming for her, then maybe I would be okay too. Maybe she had a secret to keeping her smell under wraps or something.

I leaned forward and took my mom into a big hug. "Thanks, Mom."

She sighed, her chest shaking as she held me. "Your entire job as a parent is to keep your children safe at the very least." Her voice broke. "First when you were fifteen and now...your father and I went wild when Sawyer told us the vampires had taken you."

She pulled back and there was a fierceness in her eyes, a warrior I'd never seen before. "If it happens again, your father and I will go to the ends of the Magic City looking for you and we will leave a trail of bodies in our wake, you understand me?"

My eyes widened. "Mom!"

She nodded. "That's right. I'm not some weak schoolteacher, some nice old lady. Those bloodsuckers better *watch out*."

I burst into crying laughter, the manic kind where you didn't really know whether you wanted to cry or laugh and so you did both. "I love you," I told her. It was sweet, but with her cuffs she couldn't even shift—

My mouth opened in shock as my gaze went to her wrists.

"MOM! They took off your cuffs!" My voice was colored with shock but not near as much shock as I felt. How had I just sat through an entire dinner without realizing she was cuffless? Free!

She grinned like a schoolgirl, nodding as tears shone in her eyes. "Just this morning. Sawyer had a hard time finding a witch powerful enough to work on it, one that hasn't gone against us."

I chewed my bottom lip. Was the entirety of Magic City against us now, over me? Because that was awkward as hell.

"Your father and I took a run in wolf form together

this morning." She grinned. "Happy to report I'm still faster than him."

"I tripped!" my father called from the open doorway, and I spun to see he and Sawyer making their way out into the garden. My gaze flashed to Sawyer's pockets, checking for the bulge of a ring box.

Nothing.

"Get the solar worked out?" my mom asked, her tone completely light and nonchalant, but we both watched Sawyer's face for a reaction.

My dad nodded. "It's such a fancy system, you can't even see the panels." He pointed to the roof. "They're built into the roof shingles!"

My face fell and my mom shot me a gaze that said, *I'm sorry.*

Damn.

"Ready to head back now, Demi, or would you like to spend some more time with your parents? I can come get you later, but I've got a few meetings to attend to," Sawyer said.

"I'll head back. I want to get settled in for classes tomorrow and catch up on what I missed." I gave my mom and dad big hugs, and was surprised when my mom pulled Sawyer into a hug too. After shaking hands with my dad, Sawyer led us outside, where Walsh was leaning against the front of his car. Sage was standing in front of ours looking down the street like she expected an attack at any moment.

As we approached, she gave me a small smile and then looked at her cousin. "Did you get the text about the small breach in the south wall?"

Sawyer nodded. "It's been taken care of. Group of dark fey."

The dark fey were trying to break into the south wall of Werewolf City? I gulped.

Maybe getting engaged wasn't the biggest priority right now...

CHAPTER TEN

I T WAS BACK TO CLASSES AS USUAL, AND BEING NORMAL felt great. After the first few days, people stopped staring and whispering about my "time away." Upside: no attacks in the past eight days. Downside: was Sawyer ever going to fucking propose to me? Or was it like, assumed I was going to marry him? I mean we *were* living together. He was even turning his guest bedroom into a photography studio for me while we met with an architect to build us a house on ten acres of prime Wolf City land. It felt a little surreal to be honest.

I stepped out of my final class for the day and Eugene was waiting for me. Every day after school we had driving lessons. They were normal at first, and I had totally gotten the hang of it, but then they turned into wild "defensive driving" lessons. Sometimes that meant that Sage sped up beside me on the highway and jerked into me while Eugene told me how to respond.

It was hell on my nerves, but apparently what I needed to learn to be the alpha's wife.

"What are we doing today? Driving eighty while defusing a bomb?"

Eugene's upper lip curled. "No. You're going to do a sliding parallel park without stopping."

I frowned. "A what?"

Eugene sighed as we walked across the quad. "You'll be going forty and then jerk the wheel to pull into a spot, then get out and run into a police station or whatever safety lies beyond. All within seconds."

My eyes bugged. "The hell I will."

Eugene stopped and looked at me. "When Sawyer was taken, when he was little, he was with his mother. They think the woman is the weaker link when they try to kidnap."

I growled, throaty and raw. "Eugene, I can catch bullets and go invisible. I dare them to come after my future children."

He grinned, a slow and sly full, white-toothed smile. Was that pride in his gaze? I'd always liked him.

Before he could respond, music blared into the quad over the loudspeaker. It was soft and romantic and totally weird to be played out of the school speakers. People murmured behind me and I spun to take in the scene.

My heart stopped, literally stopped in my chest, when I saw Sawyer walking toward me holding a microphone. It wasn't him, or the mic, or the music that made me stop dead, it was the custom T-shirt he wore.

"*Future Mr. Calloway-Hudson,*" it read.

I burst into giggles, but then grew serious as I realized what was happening. Was he...proposing? Was this it? Eugene stepped back with a grin as the crowd opened up.

Sawyer placed the microphone to his lips. "I am of sound mind and body, with not a single love spell in my system," he declared, and the entire student body erupted into laughter, including myself. "And I choose you, Demi Calloway. I choose you." My laughter died in my throat as he dropped to one knee and pulled a giant shiny diamond ring out of the tiny pocket in his jeans. Sans box. "I publicly humiliated you in front of everyone, and so I think it's only fair that I do the same to myself, wearing this ridiculous T-shirt."

The crowd cheered and I grinned. I loved the shirt, I loved him, I loved it all.

Sawyer looked up at me from on his knee and I peered into those bright blue eyes. "I choose you, Demi. Now, if only you will choose me back, I would be the happiest man alive. Marry me?"

Tears leaked from my eyes. He was reversing the public shame he'd caused me, and it meant everything.

Sawyer wasn't afraid to look like a fool for those he loved, and it made him more perfect than ever before.

I tapped my chin, eyeing the diamond. "I'll have to think about it."

A few students snickered, and Sawyer responded with a growl before I burst into laughter, crying. I felt ridiculous right now, going through so many emotions. "YES! It's a huge yes from me, Mr. Calloway-Hudson."

He dropped the mic on the ground as the students erupted into applause, and then he tackle-hugged me, his mouth on mine in an instant. We kissed each other hungrily before pulling away so that he could put the ring on my finger.

It was the size of a toaster.

"I know you don't care about expensive shit, but I want everyone who meets you to know how much I love you and will take care of you."

Fucking swoon.

"I love it. It's like a little extra murder weapon." I made a slashing motion through the air and he grinned. Reaching out, I tapped his shirt. "This is adorable, but you know the guy doesn't hyphenate as well, right?"

His face fell. "They don't?"

I burst into laughter, shaking my head. "Were you prepared to change your name?"

He nodded. "I was about to have the hospital renamed and everything."

Lightness flooded through my body and I just wanted

to stay in this moment forever. I grinned and he reached out and fireman lifted me, throwing me over his shoulder. "She said yes!" he screamed, and the entire school erupted into more cheers and applause.

I hated attention like this, but Sawyer thrived in this type of environment, so I was going to let him have his moment. I wanted to freeze time and stay in this perfect love bubble that Sawyer and I had created.

It wouldn't last forever, not with war brewing...but I wanted it to. I wanted marrying Sawyer to be the only thing on anyone's mind for a long time.

———·—·———

Sawyer carried me through campus over his shoulder the entire way, raising his fist to anyone who passed and screaming, "She said yes!"

It was adorable. Like baby kitten adorable. And I wouldn't take this from him no matter how much his shoulder bone was digging into my rib cage. When we reached the doorway to our shared apartment, he set me down, sliding me along the length of his body.

Reaching out, he cradled my neck in his hands.

I stared at the ring, still in shock. "I wasn't sure if you were going to propose."

"The custom T-shirt got delayed or I would have sooner."

"Seriously?"

That was the freaking hold up!

He nodded. "Seriously. Once your dad said yes, I was good to go."

I furrowed my brow. "The solar panel chat?"

He grinned. "There are no solar panels on that house."

I punched his shoulder and he laughed. "I knew it! You liars."

He unlocked the door and pulled me inside. "Your mom and you were clearly digging for information, so we had to throw you off the trail."

I shook my head incredulously, staring at his tight nipples as they cut through the custom shirt. Reaching out, I ran my fingers down his abs, passing over the T-shirt fabric. "This is incredibly sexy and you should wear it every Saturday when you make me pancakes in bed."

When my fingers reached the waistband of his jeans, I let them keep going, slipping inside his pants.

He grinned. "I'm burning it tomorrow. It was a one-time thing."

I yanked my hand from his pants and pouted.

"Yes dear, whatever you say," he amended and I laughed, pouncing on him.

I leapt up into the air and he caught me, hands around my ass as his back slammed into the wall. With a growl he threw his head back. "Woman, you'll be the death of me."

"Hope not." I licked a line down his neck. "I like you alive."

He moaned, walking forward a few steps and setting my ass down onto the kitchen counter. I reached down and yanked my shirt off in one quick move and then he leaned forward to suck my nipple through my mesh bra. You know that fake, quick, rough sex they always have in movies that you know isn't real?

It's real. Oh man it's real.

Sawyer slipped his hand up my denim skirt, tucking my panties aside, and plunged a finger inside of me, causing me to gasp out in pleasure. With the same quick movements, I reached for him, unbuttoning and yanking his pants down before grasping his hard length in my hands.

He growled in my ear, pulling a condom out of thin air. "I *need* you."

Of all the things he could have said, that's what I wanted to hear. I wanted to be needed. I liked that so much of Sawyer was wrapped up in so much of me. Without even taking off my skirt, I scooted forward on the counter and he kept my panties pulled to the side as he plunged inside of me in one quick thrust.

"Fuck," I gasped, threading my fingers through his hair and pulling hard. He leaned forward, taking my bottom lip into his mouth as I propped myself up on the kitchen counter and moved in rhythm with his thrusts. Delicious pleasure radiated through my entire body, making heat and wetness throb between my legs.

"Sawyer," I moaned.

His tongue trailed down my neck as he pumped harder and my body tightened just before the explosion.

"Don't ever leave me again," he gasped desperately against my neck.

"Never again," I promised as an orgasm ripped through my body and I cried out, Sawyer's mouth on mine swallowing my sound.

I loved him with every fiber of my being. Nothing would ever break us apart again.

———•·•———

I was in a deep sleep when a hand clamped around my mouth. I tried to scream. My eyelids flicked open and I came face-to-face with a familiar set of searing blue-teal eyes.

Arrow.

He put his finger to his lips and the scream died in my throat. Then he peeled his hand away from my mouth and nodded toward the living room.

What. The. Fuck?

My heart pounded in my throat at the sight of him. *Arrow.* A Paladin wolf. Here. In my room. Where I slept next to the future alpha werewolf! If Sawyer or Eugene found him, they would kill him first and ask questions later.

With one glance at Sawyer to make sure he was still

deep asleep, I slipped out of bed, grateful I was clothed, and hugged my arms around my chest, shaking the last vestiges of sleep from my mind. I closed the door behind me and pulled Arrow into my photography studio.

"You didn't tell me you were the future alpha's wife," he said, looking around my studio. I swallowed hard, about to answer when he spoke again. "Or a Paladin."

I froze and he spun to face me, a fierceness in his gaze that frightened me. "I can smell it on you now. Why wasn't it there before? You smell like Run, and alpha, and home." There was desire in his voice but not of a sexual nature. It was...something else. Something that was hard to explain. Like with Astra, like pack, like family.

"I was still figuring it all out for myself," I told him honestly. "And you held a gun to the back of my head."

His cheeks reddened and I wondered if he didn't smell the Paladin on me because when I met him I was wearing the cuffs. When I met Astra, who could smell it on me, I wasn't.

"My mom—"

He nodded. "The white girl Run loved. We all know the story. She got him killed."

I opened my mouth to argue, but he was right. If my mom hadn't been with Run that day in the barn...he would still be alive, but that didn't mean it was her fault.

"Why are you here? In my *home*."

He tapped the blade at his waist. "Sometimes I run

errands for the vampires, do what I have to in order to keep our people fed." Guilt layered thickly over me at that, especially when he said *our* people. "They gave me a bounty. For you."

The breath caught in my throat as my wolf surged to the surface, going semitransparent, and leapt in front of me immediately, before solidifying and giving Arrow a low, warning growl.

He watched in interest, but not shock at what my wolf could do, which meant he'd seen it before. On that girl my mom spoke about? The one who survived the fire?

"Relax," he said calmly. "If you think I'm murdering my people's last chance to claim an alpha, you're wrong."

My wolf relaxed and Arrow dropped to one knee, putting out his hand to her. She tentatively crept forward, sniffing his palm, and he pet her between the ears like you would a dog. She started to wag her tail for full effect.

'Traitor.'

'He's nice. Smells like us.'

I sighed. "You weren't surprised by her. Have you seen a split shifter before? My mom says Run told her about one."

He nodded. "We had one for a bit...we call them wolf angels."

Wolf angel. That was...beautiful and so much better than *demon*.

He said they *had* one...for a bit.

All hope that I had that she was still alive evaporated. "Did they...kill her?" I asked. Maybe the vampires got her too.

Sadness pulled at his features as he frowned. "She... killed herself. Being hunted your entire life can wear on you, ya know?"

I didn't move. Didn't breathe.

She killed herself. She would rather die than continue to be hunted. It was...a sobering reality I had never thought of. How many years could I live like this? Being kidnapped and then breaking free? Going to war over it...?

'*Don't think about that,*' my wolf snapped.

"Is it true you saved Astra? You met her?" Arrow asked, breaking my depressing inner monologue.

"Yes, but she saved my friend first."

"Then what the *snakebite* are you doing here?" he asked with a hiss, and I tried not to grin at his choice of cussword. "*Come home.* Each day we bleed magic. We need a leader to anchor our people to the land lest we become human. Don't you care?"

What? Human?

"I...don't know what you are talking about."

Arrow sighed. "Paladin alpha raised with city wolves. Perfect." He rubbed his temples.

"Paladin alpha raised with humans *actually*," I corrected. "I grew up a banished wolf in Spokane, Washington."

He groaned. "That's worse. We will lose our wolves, our magic, our pride. Everything. Demi, we are over ten thousand strong. If we die, that's on you!"

What? They would lose their wolves? Ten thousand... that was a ton...way more than Sawyer or anyone knew about, I was sure.

"I'm getting..." I held up my left hand and showed him the ring. "Married."

He frowned. "You don't understand. We are the last *true* werewolves. Magic runs through our veins. We can turn other people into werewolves by biting them. We claim our pack with pack bonds. We're...*real*. Not like these fake and weak, watered-down shifter wolves." He gestured to the door where Sawyer slept.

"Be careful how you talk about those I love," I growled.

He sighed, shaking his head. "And what of us?" he growled. "Don't you love us? We're your *real* family. Astra is your pack. If what she says is true, you've already claimed her. That means you've already taken on your position as alpha. You must come home and prove yourself before our magic bleeds into the sky and we become worthless humans!"

Holy shit. Was he serious?

"That's a lot to...digest," I said, wondering what the hell I was going to do about it.

"Demi!" Sawyer's voice called frantically from the bedroom, and Arrow started for the window of my office.

"Come home. Make Run proud. We need you."
Arrow, his eyes wide, looked at me for the first time
with vulnerability.

"In my studio!" I called to Sawyer so he didn't have
a heart attack and go on a rampage.

"I'll think about it…" I told Arrow. He leapt out
onto the open window ledge and looked back at me.

"That man that saved you from your fall, *that* was
your grandfather. Please tell me he didn't die saving
someone that was too *selfish* to help her people in a
time of need." Then he leapt out the window and took
off running the second his feet hit the ground.

His words cut right into my chest, making my soul
bleed. It was my grandfather, just as I expected.

"What are you doing?" Sawyer called from the
doorway, and I froze. He would be able to smell the
male in the room and I didn't want to lie to him. Starting
a marriage on a lie was sure to turn into a shit show of
a life.

I spun around, a tear slipping free from my cheek.
Sawyer looked at my tear, the open window, and then
my wolf, and gripped his heart. "Who was here? Tell me
you aren't cheating on me, Demi." The broken vulnerability in his voice killed me.

"Ohmygod no!" I rushed forward and then plopped
down at his feet and patted the ground next to me.
Sawyer took a seat, watching me with a pale complex-
ion and untrusting gaze. I didn't blame him.

"Sawyer...my real dad...wasn't *just* a Paladin," I breathed.

His entire body clenched and he sniffed the air, no doubt smelling a male Paladin wolf.

"He was also the alpha." I dropped the bomb and waited.

The poor guy had no idea it was coming. His entire face fell, mouth going slack. I swallowed hard. "I met a Paladin wolf named Arrow on my journey through Troll Village. He just came by to ask me to—"

"He was here in our house?" Sawyer stood, bolting from the room.

"Sawyer, wait!" I took off after him, yanking his arm.

"Demi, there could be more. They could be about to attack!" His hand was on the front doorknob to alert whatever guard stood outside this door.

"Sawyer, *listen* to me. I'm trying to tell you something important. The Paladins are *my* people. They aren't going to attack us!"

He froze, body going limp at my words and he spun from the closed front door to face me with the most hurt expression I'd ever seen. "Your people? What does that make us?"

Fuck. This was not a position I wanted to be in. "You're my person and Sage and your people are my people too." I threaded my fingers through his hair and he closed his eyes. "I just have...a lot of people...and

207

I don't want to be forced to belong to one group. It doesn't feel right."

"What did he want?" he growled.

I sighed. "For me to go to the Paladin lands and...I dunno, be their alpha, I guess. He said they needed me or their magic would die out."

He barked out a laugh, but my glare stopped him.

"I'm sorry, Demi, go live in trees and tents and be alpha of the wild Paladins? No thank you." He chuckled.

I frowned. "Have you ever even been to their land? Did Astra seem like a *wild Paladin* to you?"

He quieted. "Well, she didn't seem *normal*, and no I've obviously never been to the traitors land who *cursed my entire family*."

Shit, I'd forgotten about that. I winced.

"Well, maybe they've changed. Maybe they don't curse anymore..." I offered, knowing I was fighting a losing battle. It was totally horrible that a Paladin witch wolf, or whatever, had cursed his line and he'd had to live with the consequences.

Sawyer threaded his fingers through mine. "My darling, if you want to be an alpha, then you can lead *here* by my side. You say the word and you can be as involved in leadership as you want. You want to be on my war team? Granted. You want to start making the budget for next year? Done. But I need you *here*. With me. With your parents. Sage. *Our* people."

He was right. This was a stupid weird midnight

intrusion. What was I going to do, run off into the woods and leave my fiancé, my parents, my best friend? No way.

Arrow was trippin' if he thought that, and why come in the middle of the night with a knife on his belt after he admitted to being sent by the vampires? Maybe he was dangerous to me…

But even though I wanted to think he might be an enemy and put his plight out of my mind, I knew that couldn't be true. No…he would never hurt me. He'd gotten in my apartment where I slept with round-the-clock security. If he wanted to kill me, he would have.

"How did he get in here?" Sawyer went to the front door and pulled it open.

Our eyes fell to Walsh, passed out on the floor with some type of tranquilizer dart in his neck. Red and black feathers protruded from the end of the dart. It looked homemade.

"Bastard," Sawyer growled.

I ignored the insult. I knew he was just pissed Arrow got one up on his friend. We pulled the dart from his neck and then dragged Walsh into the living room, heaving him up onto the couch. Then Sawyer called in a replacement guard and we went back to bed.

What a night. Not how I wanted to tell Sawyer my deep dark secret. Not on the day after he proposed to me! We both lay there for an hour staring at the ceiling wide awake, that unsaid elephant hanging in the room.

I was a Paladin alpha.

Fuck.

———•·•———

The next few days, Sawyer and I tried to pretend Arrow never showed up and that I hadn't dropped the alpha bomb on him. Instead we planned for our very public, very giant, engagement party. Wolves were invited from around the entire city. My parents were guests of honor, which was going to be awkward as fuck. The last time my mom and dad had to see Curt Hudson was after he banished them. Sawyer wanted everyone who attended to know that they were forgiven, and the guest of honor position did that politically...I guess. I was still learning to be a political sleuth. It didn't suit me, but I knew it was my future.

"It has to be classy but sexy. Think of yourself like the first lady," Sage said as we roamed the mall looking for an engagement dress for myself for tonight. Yes, I was waiting until the last minute. Walsh and Eugene trailed behind us at a ten-foot pace because Sage was off duty and on bestie detail.

"I will not! Gross," I told her. "I'm the future alpha's wife. No *big deal*." I gulped.

She laughed, and laughed some more until I elbowed her in the ribs.

As we stepped into another dress shop, the hairs on

the back of my neck stood up and I suddenly had the strangest feeling I was being watched.

Glancing over my shoulder, I looked at Walsh and Eugene, and scanned the area around them. Nothing out of the ordinary. Hmm.

"I'm thinking black. It's classic," I told Sage.

She shrugged. "It's also boring. What about deep blue? Oh, or red!" She ran to a floor-length red gown with see-through side panels and stroked her fingers over the fabric.

I shook my head. "Red says I'm a siren who has entrapped your future alpha and I intend to be a conniving bitch through his entire reign."

Sage's eyes bugged out. "Wow, tell me how you really feel."

I grinned and stepped over to trail my fingers across a pale blue number. It was a muted color, but something about it reminded me of Audrey Hepburn or Marilyn Monroe; it was a classic color. I pulled it out and inspected the design. The upper bodice was a tight corset style, only belling out into a flare at the knees like a mermaid. From the knees down were tiny sewn in crystals.

"Oh, Dem, it's gorgeous." Sage ran her finger over the small satin bow under the bust.

I grinned. "I love it." Pulling the tag out, I glanced at the price and my eyes fell out of my head.

"I hate it. Let's go to another store." I went to hang it back up.

Five grand, for an engagement dress. *Were they serious?*

Sage pulled the tag from my hands and looked at it, rolling her eyes. "My sweet sixteen dress was more than this. It's totally fine."

My mouth dropped open. "Sage, that's *obscene.* That's someone's monthly salary."

She pulled out her phone and hit a few buttons.

I panicked. "No. What are you doing?" Sage was a loose cannon; I never knew what she was going to do.

"Hey, Cuz," Sage purred into the phone and my whole body went rigid. "Demi is scared to buy her dream dress for tonight because it's five grand."

I punched her in the arm, *hard*, and she winced before handing me the phone.

"You asshole," I mouthed to her, but she simply held the dress over her body and began to spin around the room with it as she ignored me.

"Hello..." I gulped, pressing the phone to my ear.

"I love that you're economical," Sawyer said, "but I plan on only getting married once, so let's go big or go home with this, okay, love?"

"I mean, I guess if there is any time to go big or go home, it's with your wedding to a millionaire." I laughed nervously into the phone. I hated talking about money. It felt weird when I stopped to think of all the stuff Sawyer bought me and how much it might cost.

"Billionaire. But yes, get the dress, okay? Can't wait to see you in it."

Billionaire. My eyes bugged and I mentally stumbled over his words. I mean I had seen Hudson on everything since I got here. Hudson hospital, Hudson laboratories, Hudson pharmaceuticals but...billionaire? I shook my head.

"Kay," I squeaked into the phone and ended the call. "Low blow," I called at Sage and chucked the phone at her. She caught it in mid-air and then laughed.

"Try it on." She shoved the pretty dress at me and I conceded.

After slipping the dress on, it was like the fashion angels sang as I walked out to model for Sage. It fit like a glove and I felt so beautiful.

Sage's mouth dropped open at the sight of me. "Holy shit. You have to wear heels with it."

I shook my head. "Sawyer said yesterday not to get shoes, that he got some for me."

Her face screwed up. "That's dangerous. If they are hideous, you will have to pretend you love them."

I grinned, about to retort when I felt something... that weird feeling I was being watched again. It was a pull on my energy that I couldn't explain, yet it felt familiar, so I was just left feeling confused.

"What's wrong?" Sage must have noticed my face.

I swallowed hard. "Nothing." I stepped into the dressing room and quickly changed, then paid for the dress with Sawyer's credit card. I wanted to be happy. Tonight was my big night, but I felt this pit in my stomach, a sickening feeling that was mixed with loneliness. I felt fine before we got to the mall, but now my emotions were all weird and depressing.

What the hell?

I was about to question my sanity, when we stepped out of the store and Astra leapt into view. "Alpha." Her voice shook as she sprang in front of me.

My heart jackknifed in my chest at the sight of the tiny Paladin wolf on Werewolf City land.

Eugene stepped forward, springing into action from across the mall, but Walsh stopped him, looking at me.

I shook my head, and then waved them off. "Sage, can you give us a moment?" I handed her my dress and she looked confusedly at Astra, nodding.

Why was she here?

The small wolf girl looked dirty, sick, confused. She had dark circles under her eyes and a network of red scars across her face; her skin was pale and covered with dirt. There were even a few twigs in her hair. A protective need surged up inside of me.

"What happened to you?" I grasped her shoulders and pulled her aside.

Had she tried to heal someone again and only taken on the illness herself?

That sick lonely feeling I'd felt in the dressing room fled me then and a resolute calm washed over me as she sighed in relief. It took me a moment to realize I hadn't been feeling my own feelings, I'd been feeling hers!

"Alpha. I *need* you," she whispered.

I frowned at her. She looked like she was in rough shape, and although she insisted on calling me that name that I hated, I didn't want her to suffer.

"What happened? How can I help you? Do you need some food? Medical care?" I gestured to the food court. She looked skinnier since I'd last seen her if that were possible. It had only been a few weeks. Had someone been starving her? Anger surged within me at the thought.

Her bottom lip quivered. "Alpha. Come *home*. Please."

Fuck. Not this again. My heart tightened in my chest until it felt like I couldn't breathe. "Did Arrow send you?"

She swallowed hard. "Arrow is off trying to make money so we can trade for food and blankets and all the things we need."

What the what did she just say? "You *all* need food?" Did all of the Paladins look like this? Had Arrow looked skinnier last time I'd seen him? I had been half-asleep and hadn't noticed, and he'd been clothed this time.

Astra placed one hand on each side of my face, and I saw Walsh, Eugene, and Sage press in closer to me, hands on their weapons.

"When will you understand? We. *Need*. You." Her voice cracked and the spots where her fingers touched my face started to tingle. "The magic that makes our people special is tied to *you*. Come. Home. Now." She growled the last word and I knew it was asking a lot of her. She was the most submissive wolf I'd ever met, and yet she stared into my eyes, holding eye contact, and it burned right through to my soul.

I swallowed hard, staring back as tears threatened to spill over, a thousand thoughts flashing through my mind. I *had* to help them. How could I not? I mean, they were people and they were suffering...but Sawyer...my love, my fiancé that I was marrying...I couldn't just leave this whole world to go live in the fucking jungle with his sworn enemy.

She broke eye contact, looking away from me and at the surrounding mall. "You're not coming." There was disappointment in her voice, finality.

"I'm going to help you," I assured her. "You remember that place we came through the Wild Lands wall into Werewolf City a few weeks ago?"

She nodded, but her shoulders drooped like she'd lost all hope.

"Go there with some of your people. Bring wheelbarrows or horses or whatever, because I'm going to have a bunch of food sent there."

She frowned, looking utterly destroyed. "Okay, Alpha."

Fuck. Why did the disappointment in her voice tear into my heart?

"Food is good. You need food, right? Oh, and blankets." I snapped my fingers. "I'll send both...okay?"

Her little mousy brown hair formed a curtain around her face. She nodded, making it shake, then her chin snapped up and her blue-eyed gaze held mine. "Arrow was right. The city has poisoned the heir of Running Spirit, granddaughter of Red Moon." She spat the words at my face, and then burst into tears, running off through the mall.

"Astra!" I shouted, taking off after her and then stopping. What was the use?

How did I get to this point? A few months ago, I was a banished wolf living in the human world, and now I had a giant rock on my finger, engaged to the alpha's son.

"What was that about?" Sage asked.

I blew air through my teeth. "Can I borrow your phone? I need to call Sawyer."

She nodded and handed me the phone. Sitting on the bench in front of the fancy dress store, I rang my future husband and prayed he would be kind to a people I knew deep down he'd grown up hating.

He picked up on the first ring. "My answer is yes. Buy that beautiful woman whatever she wants." Sawyer obviously thought it was Sage calling.

"Hey..." My voice cracked. I could have used our bond for this, but that felt weird. I'd rather talk it out and not internally jump on him.

He picked up on my mood immediately. "What's wrong?"

I sighed. "Remember the little healer Paladin that saved Walsh's life?"

Yes, I was reminding him of that fact in the hopes it would butter him up.

"Don't tell me she's in my house too?" he growled.

I winced. "No…just your mall."

"What now?" he asked.

"Sawyer, they're starving. The Paladins. She looked… like skin and bones. Sick. They need food and blankets. Something about their alpha dying has sickened their land or something. I don't know, but we can help them, right?"

He was silent for a long moment. Too long. So long that I had to pull the phone back and look at the screen to make sure the call hadn't ended.

"The entire reason there is a mating year and you had to date me with fifty other women is because of the Paladin wolves, you understand that, right? They cursed my family so horribly that we are all at risk of death every time we choose a *wife*!" He growled the last word and I knew it wasn't anger at me but at them.

I nodded. "I understand, and I'm…asking you to forgive them. Extend this olive branch. Send some rice and smoked meat and clothing and do the right thing."

"How many people need to be fed?" His voice was laced with annoyance, but underneath it, I heard a small hint of compassion.

Arrow had said they had over ten thousand the other

218

night, but I knew that figure would shock the shit out of Sawyer and also might make him fearful to keep them alive, because I was pretty sure he had no idea there were that many of them.

"A couple thousand," is all I said.

Silence again. "You know this isn't just up to me? I can do a lot without my father's input, but sending thousands of pounds of food to our sworn enemy is not one of them."

Shit. "But he hates them even more than you do. He'll let them starve!" I yelled into the phone. After what my mom was caught doing with Run during Curt's mating year, he would never throw the Paladins a kindness.

"This is asking a lot, Demi. When do they need the supplies by?"

I swallowed hard, thinking of how thin she looked. "Tonight. Now."

He sighed. "I'll call and ask my father and then call you right back."

I didn't want this to be a strain on our relationship, but I didn't see how I could let an entire people starve and not ask my fiancé for help when I knew he could give it. "Thank you. Oh, and Sawyer."

"Yes, Demi?"

"That Paladin wolf at the base of Waterfall Mountain who died trying to help me...that was the Paladin alpha, my grandfather. I'm here, right now, marrying you... because of him."

I was going to layer this guilt trip *really* thick.

Sawyer sighed. "Got it. I'll do my best to convince my father."

"I love you," I told him.

"I love you too, Demi, most of all your giant heart." Then he hung up.

I sat there for ten minutes, telling Sage what Astra said and bopping my foot up and down waiting for Sawyer's call.

"She did look ill," Sage commented, frowning.

I nodded, wondering what I would do if Curt said no. Before I could think on it, the phone rang.

I picked up quickly. "Hey."

"I'm sorry, Demi. He said no. But next year I'll be alpha and then—"

"No?" I stood, shock rushing through me.

He breathed into the phone. "He *hates* them, Demi. He said they could starve to death and die for all he cared. I tried to explain that politically it would be good to do the Paladins a favor, but—"

"Let them *starve*?" My voice went into a high-pitched shrill range.

"Demi, our engagement party is in four hours. You need to focus on—"

"I'll see you at the hotel." I hung up and turned to Sage as anger at my future father-in-law rolled through me.

"Take me to the alpha."

Her eyes widened. "What?"

"You heard me. I need to speak to my future father-in-law. Now."

"Uhhh, I don't know where he is. He could be in his office, or at a meeting, or—"

I sped across the mall to where Eugene and Walsh were watching me with concern. "Where is the alpha right now?" I asked Eugene. "I need to speak with him, and I know you have his schedule."

His eyes narrowed. "He's busy getting things ready for your engagement party."

"Where? At the hotel, then?" I asked.

"Demi, what's this about?" Eugene looked worried for me, and I hated that I had to play coy, but I wasn't sure how many people I should drop the Paladin alpha bomb on.

I shifted my stance. "I just need a word with my future father-in-law. It's a surprise for his son."

He checked his phone, tapping something out. It dinged with a response.

"He'll see you. Come on." Eugene started to walk away out of the mall and into the parking lot where my Range Rover was parked, next to an identical one that Sage and Walsh drove.

So he texted him? And he said he would see me? Under the grounds that this was a surprise for Sawyer? Surely he wouldn't have believed that after Sawyer just called him and made my request.

I guess I was about to find out.

CHAPTER ELEVEN

I DROVE ACROSS CAMPUS AND OUT OF THE STERLING Hill gates before heading into Werewolf City. Eugene sat shotgun as I passed the tall downtown buildings and made my way to the Hudson Plaza Hotel.

My driving was getting better, or so I thought, until I saw Eugene white knuckling it as he grasped the edges of his seat.

"Oh calm down, I'm not that bad of a driver," I scoffed just as a passing car honked at me.

Jerks.

Eugene chuckled. "You see that white dotted line?"

I nodded.

"You're supposed to stay on the *inside* of it."

I knew that. Obviously. But this was a damn SUV and sometimes that was hard. I swerved a little, bringing it back inside the line, and his fingers relaxed.

The hotel came into view at the end of the street then, and it was breathtaking. Over a thousand wolves had RSVP'd tonight and I was told even more would come to the wedding. That was like a small country. I didn't even know a thousand people, but Sawyer did. He knew them all. By name.

"Don't tell him what you are," Eugene said out of nowhere and I froze. "He knows you're part Paladin. Sawyer had to tell him after you were taken. But don't tell him you're their alpha."

My breath hitched in my throat. "Sawyer told you?"

Eugene shrugged. "I said I wouldn't protect you unless I knew everything. I don't like secrets. Secrets get people killed."

He was probably right. I'd asked him to stick his neck out for me and he didn't even know who he was protecting. "I'm sorry. Should have told you everything."

This man was going to be protecting my family, our future children. I didn't want there to be anything unsaid between us.

He waved me off. "You are right to guard this secret. Especially from him. That man hates Paladins more than he hates his own mother-in-law."

I grinned, because it was a funny reference, but I knew he was serious.

"You play the angle that you befriended this little Paladin girl, she saved Walsh, and now this is a political repayment. Got it?"

Damn, he knew exactly why I was going. I couldn't get anything past Eugene. "You were eavesdropping at the mall," I stated as I pulled into the valet stand at the hotel.

He shrugged. "My job. I didn't know if you were going to get emotional again and run off, only to be kidnapped by vampires." He reached out and clasped my hand. "I took your disappearance personally. I'm sorry I wasn't there to protect you."

A lump lodged in my throat as I threw the car in park. Eugene was in the ICU for four days. That's like four weeks in human time. "It's okay. It wasn't your fault."

I squeezed his hand, but he shook his head. "Agree to disagree."

My door opened and it shook me from my emotional moment.

Eugene blamed himself for my disappearance? I had no idea. Before I could say anything more, the man who opened my door bowed his head to me. "Alpha Hudson is waiting to see you, Miss Calloway."

Oh crappers.

I stepped out and followed him through the giant double doors while Eugene lingered behind me, his eyes flicking left and right like a hawk.

This place was insanely stunning. Everything looked like it was made of gold; it dripped elegance and refinery. Sawyer had taken me here two nights ago to check it out as a possible wedding venue. When I told him I loved it, he said *good*, because it was our engagement party venue as well. It was the only place able to hold over a thousand wolves. The party would be split with about four hundred in the main ballroom and then another four hundred on the outside patio and two hundred on the lawn.

The man who was leading me took a left down the hallway and then an immediate right into the giant ballroom, which was being decked out with white roses, floating lanterns, and hundreds of circular tables.

Sawyer's mom was in the middle, barking orders at a dozen servers who were ironing tablecloths. When I'd told her I wasn't really into party planning and just to do whatever she'd wanted, she'd hugged me and told me it was probably for the best, considering my wardrobe.

My gaze fell to the corner of the room. Mr. Hudson wore a black tux and leaned up against a wall, tapping out something on his phone.

"Demi! You're so early and you're...*not* ready." Sawyer's mom trailed her gaze over my messy mall hair and jeans and T-shirt.

I laughed nervously. "Got the perfect dress and I'm about to get my hair done, I just had to ask Mr. Hudson something..."

I looked over at him to find that he was watching me with an unreadable expression. He tipped his head to a back room. I swallowed hard and followed him.

"Don't be long! That hair needs help," Mrs. Hudson called after me cheerily.

That woman was a 1950s housewife, I swear. The man who had been leading me through the entire hotel now stopped and just let me walk into the room alone while Eugene took watch outside the door with another man I didn't recognize. There were so many guards now, it was hard to keep track.

I shut the door behind me and readied my speech. Mr. Hudson seemed like a reasonable man and—

"I already told Sawyer no. We are not helping the Paladins. They can starve and do us all a favor." He continued to tap on his phone without looking up at me.

My eyes went wide at his nonchalant behavior over the situation.

"But, sir—"

"Is that all? Because my answer is final, and I'm very busy getting everything paid and set up for tonight."

So he was going to play the money card? Try to make me feel bad that I couldn't afford to pay for my own wedding? That stubborn *bastard*. I strode across the room and ripped his phone out of his hands, forcing him to look up at me in shock.

"I'm sorry I'm poor and can't pay for all of this," I growled. "Maybe if you hadn't *banished* my mother she could have provided a better life for me." Immediately I regretted my temper.

He looked at me with a mixture of pride and anger.

"God, you're just like her. You *look* just like her too."
He looked at the wall before meeting my gaze again and
I realized he was talking about my mother. Is that why
he barely ever looked at me?

"Sir, please. They are starving," I pleaded.

He chuckled.

"*Good.* Karma for cursing my family with a death
curse for the past thousand years!"

"Exactly!" I yelled, matching his tone and not even
caring that this shit show had completely gone off the
rails. "It was a thousand years ago! Get over it!"

He barked out a laugh at my bold statement and
then shook his head at me. "Listen, Demi. I am still in
charge for the next year or so, and I will make it my *last*
order of business to make sure that no help ever goes to
the Paladins from my hand."

I dropped his phone on the desk and put my hands
on my hips. "You would let thousands die because
you're still pissed my mom loved a Paladin before she
even met you?"

Rage threaded into his eyes, yellow and orange
bleeding through his blue until I was staring at his wolf.

"Your mother is my Meredith," he said, and I
frowned.

"What?"

He took in a deep breath and then released it, the
colors in his eyes going back to blue. "She publicly
humiliated me, just as Meredith did to you, and I'll

never forget that feeling. I...loved her. I wanted to spend the rest of my life with her, and if she didn't want that, she should have dropped out of the mating year."

Ouch. I knew what he was saying but he was wrong.

"Meredith didn't humiliate me. Your son did. And you're right, my mother should have dropped out, but she was poor and you dangled a free education carrot right before her nose. What did you expect?"

He looked at me like I was some wild beast who'd come in and attacked him. "People don't talk to me like this." He sounded flustered.

I imagine they didn't. Everyone was scared of the alpha, even a timid one like him.

"I'm not afraid of you, sir. I want to have a good relationship with you. I want us to be a happy family. I want to give you grandkids and watch you play with them and invite you over for dinner without unsaid words between us. I want to be authentic around you. But you're wrong on this. The Paladins aren't your enemy."

He opened his mouth to speak and I stopped him with my hand. "They're not. Some old half witch from a thousand years ago is. They're weak, they're starving, and they're paying for a thousand-year-old mistake. We have extra food to spare. I cannot sleep at night knowing that a few miles away, thousands of wolves are slowly dying when we could help them."

He sighed. "I'm glad Sawyer chose you. He'll need a

strong woman to keep him in line if he is to be a success-ful alpha during these precarious times."

I was going to take that as a compliment. He reached up and rubbed his temples. "You had to dangle my future grandchildren in front of me, didn't you?" He grinned.

A smile pulled at my lips. "Just keeping it real, sir."

"That healer Paladin must have really made an impression on you."

Astra. Oh yes. That's why he thought I was so passionate about helping the Paladins.

I nodded. "She's barely sixteen and skin and bones. She risked her life to save Walsh in the dark fey lands."

He rubbed at his face some more. "If I do this, it sends a message to our people. I cannot cover up this big of an operation. The food trucks, the military presence needed, it can't be covered up. People will think the Paladins are no longer our enemy."

"Well, sir, last I checked everyone else was against us. Maybe we have enough enemies? Maybe it's time to make allies."

He groaned, "All right, Demi. Just this once."

I flew across the table and hugged him with a squeal of happiness. His entire body froze for a moment, like he wasn't sure how to hug someone, and then his arms came around me.

"Okay, okay. Go do the girly things while I work on this." He let me go and I pulled back with a grin.

"Thank you, sir." I turned on my heel and all but

skipped out of the room. Hopefully, this would hold off the Paladins for a week, maybe two, until they could figure out another solution.

"Demi?" Curt called from the desk.

I looked over my shoulder at him and he was smiling. "I'm glad it's you that my son is marrying. Since that first day at Delphi, when Sawyer told me he'd fallen in love at first sight with a blond goddess, I knew it was your mother's daughter. She was the only wolf I'd outcasted in my entire term as alpha."

Love at first sight? He told his dad that?

Swoon.

Curt continued: "I was so worried you'd hurt him, that you wouldn't love him back and he'd be thrust into a marriage of convenience for the sake of the curse."

Ouch. Is that what it was like for him? He was always super nice to Mrs. Hudson, but did he love her? Maybe not like he'd loved my mom.

"Unrequited love is no good for anyone," he muttered.

Damn, his face looked like a lost little boy in that moment, and I fully understood how badly this curse had hurt his family. For generations, they were forced into marriages that wouldn't have naturally occurred.

He shook himself. "Anyway, I see you two together and I know you will have a long and happy life together." He smiled.

It was actually one of the sweetest things he could have said.

"We will," I assured him. "As long as he understands happy wife, happy life."

I pointed to the custom T-shirt I was wearing that Sage got me.

He chuckled, shaking his head. "Get outta here."

A grin pulled at my lips once more. "Thanks again."

As I stepped out of the room, I couldn't help but remark that this went way better than I could have hoped. I had mad love and respect for my future father-in-law now and understood that humans were just flawed creatures, all trying to make our way through heartache and trauma. But I wanted to have a real relationship, and real people argued and aired out their grievances. I wanted to be able to go to my father-in-law with things when they bothered me and not be shut out. He'd listened to me and we'd come to an agreement, and damn that felt good. I left the hotel in high spirits.

"He's soft on you," Eugene commented as I skipped back to the car.

"Hah. That was soft? He reamed me at first," I told him.

Eugene chuckled. "He always wanted a daughter, you know. After the death of Sawyer's twin...they tried again and again and again but...to no avail." I stopped in my tracks, frowning.

The curse. It only let you have two children, and when Sawyer's twin brother died...they weren't allowed to have any more. No wonder he hated the Paladins. It took his chance at being able to have a daughter.

"That's really sad," I said.

"That's life," he retorted.

No truer words were spoken.

CHAPTER TWELVE

I STEPPED INTO THE LITTLE PRIVATE ROOM THAT THE hotel had set up for family so that we could all enter the main ballroom together. We were a bit early, but Sawyer was already inside because he'd texted me as much on my new phone, which he'd had delivered to my hair salon.

After unwrapping it, I'd promptly taken a selfie and posted it on my Insta.

"I need a doctor!" Sawyer clutched his heart in mock agony as I walked into the room in my new dress, hair spun up in a cascade of glossy curls. "I'm marrying the most beautiful girl in the world and I can't breathe."

I grinned. "You're a charmer, you know that?"

He straightened, pulling his hand away from his chest, and pulled me into his arms, my body pressed flat against him. "You bring it out of me."

Sage made a mock retching noise behind us and I spun around to flip her off, only to catch Walsh totally checking out her ass. His eyes snapped up to mine when he caught me looking, cheeks going red, and I grinned.

When I spun back around, Sawyer released me and pulled two boxes from a nearby table, handing them to me. "Engagement gift."

My eyes widened. Shit, was that a thing? "I...didn't get you anything."

He waved me off. "You're my gift. You even wore a bow." He fingered the bow under the bust of my dress.

I grinned and then tore into the first present. I hated surprises but I loved presents. Who didn't? When my gaze landed on the pair of white Converse sneakers encrusted with thousands of tiny rhinestones, I squealed.

"Oh my God, you are so not wearing those." Sage peeked over my shoulder and Sawyer flicked the top of her head, lightly pushing her back.

I laughed as she flipped him off, and then I kicked off my flip-flops and slipped on the little thin socks he'd provided and the shoes.

"They're my most cherished possession," I told him, and looked up to see him grinning, dimple and chin butt on full display.

"Second gift now." He cleared his throat, suddenly looking nervous. He met Sage's gaze and she nodded, walking to the other side of the room with Walsh to give us privacy.

My stomach churned with excitement, ripping off the wrapping paper. I pulled away the lid of the box.

When my eyes fell on the pair of metal cuffs, my heart sank into my stomach.

"No." Not again. He wouldn't...

Panic seized me, and Sawyer grasped the sides of my face lightly. "This isn't what you think. Well, it is, but these are cuffs you can take on and off at will. No magic or fey blade needed, and they do not shock you. They only shut off your magic and hide your scent."

I released the breath I'd been holding. "How?" I stroked the cuff, inhaling and smelling the magic on them.

"I commissioned them months ago, before the witches turned on us. Now if you want to hide your powers, you can, and if you need your wolf, you just slip them off. Like jewelry."

They were metal inside, but black leather outside with braided detailing, fashionable.

Tears filled my eyes. The gift was so thoughtful. After everything we'd been through together, and everything I'd been through...he gave me a choice, a choice in my life and how I wanted to live it.

"Thank you." A tear slipped down my cheek.

"Stop crying! Makeup," Sage piped up from the corner of the room and I laughed.

Sawyer leaned down to brush his lips against mine. "I just want you to be safe on your own terms."

I growled throatily. "That's the sexiest thing you've ever said to me."

He then moved to my ear. "Tonight I'm going to rip this five-thousand-dollar dress off of you before we even reach the kitchen," he whispered.

A warmth pulsed inside of me as a smirk pulled at my lips. "Promise?" I whispered back, and he moaned, low and seductive.

"Parents incoming," Sage warned, and we both broke apart smiling. The doors opened and my mom and dad entered wearing the loveliest clothes I'd ever seen them in.

"Holy crap." My jaw unhinged at the sight of my mother in a deep blue dress and then my father in a black suit and blue tie.

My mom did a full spin and my dad catcall-whistled her.

I gave them a hug, and we made small talk for a few moments when Sawyer's dad and mom entered the room. True to his word, the alpha had delivered thousands of pounds of dry food and extra blankets to the meeting space I told him about, and Astra was on hand with Arrow and a bunch of others to receive the shipment. Sawyer texted me a picture to show me while I was getting my hair done. They'd loaded the stuff into wheelbarrows and carts pulled by donkeys, while some just carried huge sacks of rice on their backs.

Curt cleared his throat, and the intensity of the

236

moment when my mom and him would see each other again was palpable. Sawyer's mom had a tight smile, clearly uncomfortable while his dad was just completely void of emotion, his face a blank slate.

"Hello, Mr. and Mrs. Calloway, glad to have you here," Curt said and shook my father's hand. He might have included my mother in that greeting but didn't even look at her. I knew now that it was because it would hurt too much, *not* that he was being rude.

"Thank you, sir. Glad to be here and very happy for the children." My dad looked at Sawyer with his arm wrapped around me.

Sawyer's mom came over and gave us each a cheek kiss, stopping to admire my hair. "It's a miracle," she said with a wink, and I grinned. I was starting to get used to their personalities. Sawyer's mom cared about appearances and things looking pretty and I could respect that. She was also a bit of a joker.

"Thank you for inviting me, Curt." My mom's voice was small, apologetic.

Me. Not us. She was, in her own way, trying to make amends.

He finally looked at her then, and my heart broke when I saw the regret in his eyes. He didn't say anything, he just cleared his throat and nodded once.

"Shall we?" He gestured to the small door that led to the open ballroom beyond. We nodded, slipping our arms into the crook of our dates' elbows.

My poor mom. Poor Curt. Hopefully, time would heal the wounds between them. Eugene spoke into his cuff link with some CIA type move and opened the door.

The roar of the crowd was deafening and pulled me from my thoughts about my mom and Curt. I could hear the party guests before I saw them, which made nerves shoot up my spine. How many were there? Would they all be staring at me? Could any of them smell the Paladin on me? Maybe I should have slid on the cuffs rather than leave them in the box back there in the room.

Before I could obsess about it too much, Sawyer pulled me out into the crowd, which had parted, and I threw a smile on my face.

'*Holy shit, they're all here for us,*' I told Sawyer using our mental link, scanning the giant crowd.

He chuckled.

'*It's weird,*' I told him.

'*It's normal. You just don't like being the center of attention,*' he said.

True. '*I need a T-shirt for that. Don't look at me, act cool. I'm only here for the food.*'

Sawyer chuckled again and I scanned the faces of everyone here. I recognized exactly five people. Two teachers and two students and—

'*Why the fuck is Meredith's mom here!*' I shouted so loud in Sawyer's head that he winced.

Darth Vader's mom was aptly wearing a blood-red dress, glaring at me from near the champagne fountain.

Sawyer looked confused as to why I would ask that and then he nodded. '*Oh, Meredith confessed to the whole thing. The necklace with the love spell in it, hiring the guy to drink the potion and look like me. It was all Meredith.*'

I stopped walking and turned to stare at him. '*No, I saw Meredith's face when that guy turned back into his normal self. She looked shocked. Maybe the necklace was from her, but not the guy and not the vampire ambush.*'

He frowned. '*You think her mom actually sent the vampires to kidnap you?*' He stopped, something coming over his face as if it just dawned on him. '*She knew you were going to run after I chose her daughter, she knew where your dorm was, which is where the vampires took you from. She—*'

A shrill scream tore through the space and we both turned to the sound.

Oh no.

Over a hundred blurs of black-clothed figures dropped from the ceiling and into the room. The scent hit my nose then, like a shield had been lifted that once masked it and was now removed.

Copper.

Blood.

Death.

Vampire.

Chaos erupted in the room as the entire security

team at the perimeter of the building started to move to the center where the alpha was and surround him. Sawyer ripped his tuxedo jacket off and then his shirt started to split. I blinked and his giant gray wolf was now standing before me, hackles raised. I'd never seen him shift so quickly.

'*My mom!*' I looked around the room, trying to find my mom and dad. Everything was happening so fast. They had only just started shifting again, they weren't fighters. I wasn't sure they'd be able to protect themselves. I spotted them, and Sawyer and I moved as one. If I moved to the left, he moved with me. When I ran through a throng of screaming and scared partygoers, his fur was pressed into my leg.

I reached my mom in record time, which happened to be behind the wall of security that had formed around Curt Hudson. They stood in front of us like sentinels while the vampires slowly worked their way to the back of the room where we were clustered. They tossed a few wolves out of the way but hadn't engaged in full-on fighting yet.

"Get behind me," I told my parents.

"Honey—"

"Get behind me!" I growled again, my eyes going yellow as my wolf pounded my chest like a drum. She wanted to be free, she wanted to wipe the floor with these motherfuckers, but I was trying to keep her calm.

Outing myself as not only a Paladin wolf, but also a

split shifter, would put me in danger, right? But what if someone got hurt and I could prevent it?

'Just stay human for now. Let's see how this goes,' Sawyer said, reading my emotions, and I sighed in relief to have another opinion.

He was right. They hadn't attacked yet; they might just be here to send a message. Although a hundred vampires sent to the alpha's son's engagement party was quite the message in and of itself.

The lead vampire was one I recognized, a female who worked directly under the queen. I'd seen her that first night when they'd attacked Sawyer, Eugene, and I at his apartment, and then again when I was kidnapped. She was a bad-looking bitch with an upturned lip, and constantly wore a scowl.

"The queen has a message for you," she said to Curt, who stood behind a barricade of guards as we stood just beyond them with the wall at our backs.

She grinned. "An eye for an eye."

I frowned, trying to figure out what that meant, when Curt turned, panic in his gaze. He looked at Sawyer's wolf and screamed.

Everything happened in slow motion then. Curt started to run toward Sawyer's gray wolf, as I slowly turned down to look at my man. When I saw the red laser sniper dot on his wolf's chest, my whole body seized up. I moved to fall forward and throw myself in front of him, but it was too late. The sound of a high-powered rifle cut through the space, echoing off of all four walls with a sharp snap.

Blood marred the floor and my legs went weak as I fell forward and caught the alpha.

Curt lurched into my arms, blood dribbling out of his mouth as we both collapsed onto the floor.

They shot the alpha...

They'd been trying to kill Sawyer, but his dad...a sob formed in my throat. War broke out in the ballroom, the sounds of fighting and snarling and screams filled the hall, but all I could do was look into the deep blue eyes of my future father-in-law as he smiled up at me. A thin trail of blood exited his mouth and trickled down his cheek.

"No!" Sawyer shifted to human form and collapsed beside me onto his knees. "Dad!"

"Get a doctor!" Eugene yelled.

A doctor couldn't save this, nor could shifter healing. I knew by the amount of wet warmth pooling onto my thighs as his body lay draped over my lap that it was too late. He'd taken a bullet for his son, and for that I would be forever grateful.

Sawyer's mom's shrill and horrific screams filled the ballroom as she fell to the floor at her husband's side. He reached out to her, lungs gurgling with each shallow breath. "I...didn't love you, at...first," he admitted, and we all held our breath. "But I grew to love you...very... deeply, my sweet love."

She sobbed, clutching his hand and rocking back and forth. Tears rolled down my cheeks and I wished we could get Astra here, but there was no time...we were out of time.

Curt then looked at his son. Sawyer's mouth was turned into a frown, but his face was void of all emotion. He was stuck in shock, I could feel it through our bond, he couldn't believe this was happening.

"My son..." His chest rattled and Sawyer let out a strangled moan. "I'm...so proud of you." Curt took in a deep, wet breath. "You'll make ten times the...alpha I was. Especially with Demi...at your...side." He looked to me and I squeezed his other outstretched hand.

His eyes grew glassy as they began to look around the room. I thought he might just be dying, but then his gaze snapped to my mother's teary face.

"Cora," he whispered.

My mom fell to her knees, squeezing into the space between me and Sawyer, and took Curt's face in her hands. "I'm so sorry for how I treated you," she told him, looking him right in the eyes. "I should have been honest from the start and never entered the mating year."

He nodded, pulling his hand from mine and stroking her pale cheek. "Forgiven." He drew a long rattling breath then...and never exhaled. His chest just froze in place and Sawyer's mom's scream turned into a wolf's howl halfway through as she shifted mid-yell.

Holy fuck. He was dead. Sawyer's dad...our alpha. Dead.

"Sniper has been taken out. They've locked us in the room though." Eugene's voice came from above us and I realized he was talking to Sawyer. "What do we do, sir?"

He was avoiding looking at Curt's dead body, which now lay in my lap, cutting off the circulation to my legs.

Sir. He just called Sawyer "sir" because he was now the alpha...

Sawyer shook himself, taking one last look at his father. "How many guards do we have and how many of them are there?"

"Thirty of us that are trained, eighty or so of the bloodsuckers. Two hundred guests made it in before the door got sealed. The rest are on the balcony having refreshments, I presume."

Sawyer rubbed his temples as the sound of screams filled the space. Our fucking wedding guests were being slaughtered alive.

"Get the women and children and elderly in a corner and put twelve men on them to protect them. Send the rest with me to kill these bloodsuckers."

Anger surged inside of me so hot and fast that I knew I wasn't going to be able to sit this one out. "No. Take *all* of the guards with you and I'll protect the women and children," I told Sawyer as I slid his father's body off my legs and ripped the bottom half of my mermaid dress off in one jerking motion. The bloody fabric fell to the floor so that I was now wearing a minidress with my bedazzled Converse sneakers.

"Demi, I—"

"Sawyer, *fuck* hiding what I am. People are going to die!" I growled. And I was capable of catching bullets, yet I wasn't able to for his father, something I had to live with for the rest of my life now. He knew how powerful I was, he knew I was an asset, he just needed to get over his urge to treat me like glass.

"All right," Sawyer breathed. "But be safe." Then he shook himself, shifting into a gray wolf in seconds.

He looked up at me. *'I can't live without you too.'*

'I got this,' I told him, my heart breaking for his loss as I finally released my wolf. It had never been so easy. She'd been waiting just at the surface.

As the spectral wolf climbed out of my body, I heard a dozen gasps. My mother, my father, Mrs. Hudson, and anyone else who was looking at me. When my wolf solidified next to me, she looked up at me and I nodded once.

"Demon," someone from the crowd hissed.

"Paladin," another said.

I ignored them both and started to grab women and young ones and herd them to the corner of the room where the alpha had died. My mom and dad dragged Curt's body to the corner of the room, where my dad laid his jacket over his face.

"Women, children, and elderly, get to that corner of the room." Eugene pointed to where I stood, and I felt electricity dance on my skin as the vampires moved toward the corner.

Not on your fucking life, bloodsuckers.

I needed to protect this corner so that all of our guards were freed up to help Sawyer. Something cold and hard slipped into my hand and I looked up to see Sage. Her face was tracked with tears, red hair pulled from its tight bun. Her uncle had just died, and I knew she was sad, but she looked pissed as all holy hell too.

"These bloodsuckers messed with the wrong family," she growled.

I looked into my hand and grinned at the silver stake she'd placed in it. Women, children, and hobbling elders ran to our corner of the room as a bloody battle unfolded before us. My wolf held the front of the line, hackles raised.

"Honey..." My dad's worried voice came from behind me. "Do you need my help?"

I shook my head. "Keep mom safe. We got this."

The first wave of vampires came. Five at a time, and for a split second I was scared to fully give into my powers, scared to know what I was capable of and scared to show them off in front of everyone. But that moment passed and then I just wanted revenge.

Our alpha was dead, and they would pay dearly.

My wolf acted first, running out to meet the first

bloodsucker. She leapt into the air blindingly fast and attached herself to his shoulder, biting into it. My human half gripped the stake in my fingers and then fully let go of all of my powers. I let go of fear, my shame. Bolting forward so fast that everything blurred around me, I stabbed one of the vampires in the chest, killing him instantly before he could even track my movements. Then I moved to the next. Stab. Stab. I was a machine, beating them at their game, using my speed against them. I took two more down when I heard Sage scream.

Spinning around, I realized I'd gotten too far away from the ones I was supposed to be protecting. A dozen vampires were descending on Sage and my father, who'd stepped out to help hold them back. My wolf was halfway to running back to be with them, but she wouldn't make it in time. A dozen vampires against Sage and my dad were not odds I wanted.

Panic welled inside of me and I screamed, thrusting my hands out and unleashing wild, unrestrained magic in the direction of the vampires' backs.

A force shot out of me and they went down like bowling pins, like an unseen wave had completely knocked them forward. They tripped and fumbled, pinned to the floor by an unseen force.

My magic.

Holy mother. I did that...

Without overthinking it or worrying too much about the shocks and gasps around me and my freaky power, I lurched forward with my wolf and leapt in tandem over their bodies writhing on the floor, pulling against the power that held them down. When I hit the ground on the other side, I spun and held my staked fist out, as if this alone would keep them at bay.

My gaze flicked to the rest of the room, quickly taking in the scene. Sawyer and his guards were doing okay, but they had their hands full. This was all on me and Sage.

I wasn't sure how to use my powers yet, so I didn't even know how to replicate what I'd just done. I needed practice. *So much* more practice.

I also needed to get these people out of the room so they were out of harm's way and I would be free to help Sawyer and his men fight. But they'd barred the doors...

Think. Think. Think.

It came to me in a vision.

Fire.

Flames flickered in my mind's eye and I looked at Sage. "I need fire," I told her.

She didn't question it, just took off running to another corner of the room.

The vampires were starting to stand now. Whatever effects my magic had that pinned them to the floor, was wearing off.

I took a second to glance behind me. There was a window, a beautiful window with stained glass.

"Dad, break the window and get them out," I told him.

He gave me a quick nod, and without even protesting he walked over to the window and kicked it until it shattered. A little girl started to weep, clinging to her mother, and I gripped the stake in my hand, wishing I had another, or Marmal's shotgun. I vowed in that moment to never leave the house without two stakes on me at all times from now on.

The vampires popped up to their feet one by one and I rushed forward, slamming the stake into the chest of the one nearest me. The network of veins in his face immediately turned black, and I was just about to pull the stake out and kill another one when I felt two hands wrap around my throat from behind, then another set wrapped around my upper arms. Two very strong bloodsuckers pinned me to the spot as I bucked in their arms and struggled to breathe.

"Demi!" My mom's bloodcurdling scream ripped through the sounds of fighting.

'Why is your mom screaming? I can't see you.' Sawyer's panicked voice broke through my muddled mind as I thrashed in the vampires' arms like a fish out of water.

'Nothing. I'm fine,' I lied. I didn't want him worrying about me when I knew he had his own issues to focus on.

Okay, being choked out by two vampires. Don't panic, just think...

Air.

I need fucking air! The only thing I could think of was just to go limp and play dead. I went fully relaxed in their grip, letting go as my legs and everything went weak so that they had to hold me up. It worked. The pressure on my neck eased.

"The queen wants her alive," one of the vampires hissed.

That's when I exploded. Whipping my head back, I cracked my skull into the vampire behind me and internally shrieked in joy at the sound of breaking bones. Gulping deep lungfuls of air, I spun out of the other dude's grip just in time to see Sage holding a man-made torch made from a ripped curtain and a bottle of liquor. My wolf was at her side.

Thank God.

We all burst into action. My wolf leapt to rip out one of the vamp's throats, while Sage threw the bottle of liquor at the nearest vampire's chest with a battle cry.

It exploded, sending liquid and bits of glass raining down around him.

"Torch him!" I yelled. This was war, you didn't stop, you didn't think, you just reacted.

She tipped the flaming curtain torch forward and he tried to back up, but I was behind him, and lifting my bejeweled sneaker into the middle of his back, I kicked him forward and into the flames.

His body ignited and started smoking a black, thick, inky plume as he fell to the ground. I pointed to the right side of the room. "Burn that table. The ceiling sprinklers will kick on before the entire building goes up, but we can chuck bloodsuckers in the flames and even the score."

Sage grinned. "I like how you think."

We had no weapons, this was a freaking engagement party, not a war zone; we'd been ill-equipped for such an attack. Sage pulled a small bottle of liquor from her belt and grinned at me. "Cheers."

She chucked the bottle at the most beautiful table décor I'd ever seen and then tossed the torch.

The table burst into flames four feet high, and just in time.

"Demi!" my dad yelled.

I spun to the window to see he was trying to get Mrs. Hudson outside. She looked like she'd fainted and had completely lost consciousness. She was in her human form, naked and limp in my father's arms. I followed his gaze to see that a vampire had shown up and backed my mom into a corner. She was in wolf form, hunched over the alpha's dead body, hackles raised.

I'd never seen my mom's wolf in person. Only in pictures. She was stunning, strong and absolutely feral in this moment. I knew she would protect Curt's remains so that he could have a proper burial. And she would probably die for it.

My dad looked like he was about to drop Mrs. Hudson halfway out the window and run to my mom.

"Got it!" I yelled to him and burst forward. One second I was standing with Sage near the flaming table and the next I was on the vampire's back, squeezing the bloodsucker around the middle until I heard his ribs snap.

I didn't know what came over me, but I was strong, really strong. I heaved him up into the air as he kicked and hissed like a toddler having a fit.

"Mom, go!" I growled at her, unsure how long I could hold him.

My mom's wolf just looked up at me in shock, mouth opening and closing like a fish out of water. That's when my wolf appeared. She nipped my mom on the neck like a mother would to a cub, and dragged her to the window where my dad was waiting.

Plumes of gray smoke swirled in the air and I spun. The entire hall had filled with smoke now. Oops. Didn't think this through, but maybe it would force them to open the damn doors.

Screams rang throughout the space and I couldn't tell if it was their people or ours. The dude in my arms was bucking with so much force that it rocked me backward. I started to run with him in my arms, wobbly and off-balance, when I looked ahead of me and saw Sawyer and Walsh. They were tossing vampires into the bonfire like they were skipping rocks on a lake.

Horrifying and genius. I was so going to need therapy for this.

The fire alarm finally sounded, shrill and loud, and I winced, unable to hold the vampire much longer as my arms burned with fatigue.

"You'll die for this, bitch! She'll drain you, she'll—" The vamp's words were cut off when Sawyer appeared out of nowhere and throat punched the guy, collapsing his trachea. Sawyer grabbed his legs and I relaxed my hold on his ribs, letting him sink into my arms as I hooked my hands under his armpits.

'Chuck him,' Sawyer growled as the vamp thrashed and coughed in our grip.

With one swing, we arced him back and then let him loose to fly through the air and land right on the flaming inferno. He hit the table and it cracked in half as he was consumed by the flames. His screams would haunt my dreams forever, but somehow I turned off that emotional part of me and stayed in battle mode as I scanned the crowd. Most of the guests were exiting through the window my dad had bashed out, but there were still a good hundred people to get out.

"How many more vamps are there? I need to carry more stakes. I need a gun, or a sword. We need..." I couldn't think straight as the trauma of the night hit me dead on. My fists balled as I scanned dead body after dead body. Most were them. Some were us.

Oh God, Sawyer's dad. A sob ripped through my throat, which turned to a cough as the smoke hit my face.

Sawyer was wearing torn pants and no shirt. He stepped forward then and took my cheeks into his palms, pressing his forehead to mine. "It's over, Demi. That was the last one. We're safe now."

The sprinklers finally kicked on then and everything was drenched with a downpour of water that felt like someone had turned a garden hose on us. It pelted my skin in cold, hard droplets that caused me to suck in a breath in shock.

"It's over?" I whimpered, unable to meet his eyes.

His body shuddered and he pulled me into him, holding me as I cried. "Your dad, Sawyer. I'm so sorry."

His chest shook as he tried to breathe, but it turned into a cough as more smoke wrapped around us.

Walsh appeared beside us suddenly. "Let's get out of here." He yanked us toward the window. Sage appeared by my side with my wolf and I nodded to them both.

When I looked to the corner where Sawyer's dad's body should have been, I saw that it was gone. I knew that my mom and dad had taken it; they wouldn't leave him behind. I stood numbly at the back of the line while our guests crawled out a broken window of a multi-million-dollar hotel with a fire alarm blaring in the background. This wasn't how this day was supposed to go. Holy shit, this was the worst engagement party in the history of parties.

"Why won't the doors open? Can't our people on

the other side open them?" Sawyer growled as it was finally our turn to exit the building.

Eugene was here now, covered in black, goopy blood and sporting a nasty gash on his arm. "They welded them shut with steel, sir. In a manner of seconds. This was highly coordinated. Looks like they had a tip-off."

Sawyer frowned. "You think it was an inside job?"

Eugene nodded. "They knew the time, the place, the room."

Sawyer and my eyes met at the same time. "I want you to detain Mrs. Pepper for questioning," he growled.

Eugene nodded and leapt through the open window, scanning the crowd for Meredith's mom.

When we finally got through the window and stepped onto the grass lawn, one by one our guests clapped. Not a joyous exuberant clap, just a slow, weird, I'm glad you're not dead clap.

Walsh elbowed Sawyer who looked back at his best friend, confused.

Walsh puffed his chest up. "Your new alpha, Sawyer Hudson," he said as if presenting him to a royal court or something.

Oh shit.

Sawyer was the alpha now. How did that work? One died and the other just...

It seemed to dawn on Sawyer at the same time it dawned on me.

'You're alpha. Say something,' I told him.

He swallowed hard, his eyes flicking to a tree where his father lay at the base covered in a jacket, while his mother wept over his body wearing some random dude's shirt. My mom rubbed small circles on her back.

This was so wrong. How had this gone so wrong?

Sawyer closed his eyes for a moment, seemingly regaining composure, and when they opened they were bright yellow and pissed as all hell. "My father's death will be avenged." His voice was deep and raspy, heavy with his wolf. "The vampires have waged war, and it's a war I intend to win."

The clapping resumed and some of the men even cried out in agreement, but the children just clung to their mothers. How long had it been since they'd seen war? A hundred years? No one alive here surely. Certainly not my generation.

The mothers with children started taking their little ones around the side of the building for home. It was horrible to hear their screams. I knew this day would be imprinted on all of us forever.

We're all in shock, I thought. *My father-in-law is dead under a tree and I'm in shock.*

People stared at us and I wondered if we looked as horrible as we felt when I heard a whisper.

"Cursed one," someone said, and that's when I realized that my wolf was right beside me.

Shit. Everyone had seen me split shift. As if she wanted to throw it in their faces again, my wolf went

256

semitransparent and leapt into my chest, causing people to fall backward in shock, and gasp.

Well, there was no hiding what I was, and I didn't want to anymore.

"Yes, Demi is a split shifter. She's also my future wife so...get over it," Sawyer snarled, and alpha power leaked out of him and slammed into the people, causing a few to stagger backward. Some of the onlookers bowed their heads, looking to the ground in submission, but a few still stared.

"You're marrying a Paladin! Split shifters can only be Paladin wolves," a man growled.

Everyone gasped at that, and I was guessing not a lot of people knew that little tidbit of info. This was going to go off the rails really quickly if we didn't rein it in.

Sawyer opened his mouth to speak, when my mother stepped into the center of the crowd. "I met Demi's Paladin biological father when I was a young girl. He lived on the border to my gran's farm, and we were best friends since childhood."

People fell silent, looking at my mom with curiosity.

"Then he grew into a young man and I fell in love with him," she declared boldly.

Every single woman gasped as if my mom had just admitted to a murder or something equally shocking. I didn't like the way they looked at my mom, like she was a slut, so I decided to top her story with one of my own.

"Then at fifteen I was gang-raped by four vampires,"

I said, and everyone fell silent, mouths popping open in shock. "I was banished, so I had my cuffs on. Couldn't shift and protect myself."

Hands went to mouths, people openly cried out, and it was the most uncomfortable moment of my life, but I pressed on, swallowing hard as Sawyer's hand slipped in mine. "And I blacked out, but my wolf was able to split off from my body and save me."

Grown men had tears in their eyes, and women wept openly, causing me to squirm under their gaze.

"So I am who I am. Demon. Cursed one. Split shifter. Whatever you want to call me is fine, just leave my family and loved ones out of it."

Sawyer nodded. "All right, you've heard your gossip for the night. Go on home now."

He raised his arms to shoo our wedding party away, but then the women started to drag their husbands and line up single file in front of us.

What were they doing?

The first one was a woman I didn't know, about thirty years old. Her hair was drenched from the sprinklers and her mascara ran down her face in two thin black streaks.

"I'm sorry that happened to you. Thank you for protecting us tonight." She reached out and grasped my hand, giving me a small bow before leaving.

My throat tightened as the next woman stepped up. "Oh, honey, we shouldn't have judged you. I had no idea." Her voice broke as she stepped forward and pulled me into a tight hug. "Happy engagement, dear," she whispered before pulling away.

Then another and another. These women formed a line, and one by one apologized for their treatment of me, or simply said they were sorry for what happened to me, or some said nothing at all, just a hand squeeze or a hug, or a thanks for inviting them.

I chewed the inside of my cheek raw to keep from bursting into tears until the very last woman, an old lady about eighty, came up to me hobbling on a cane. Sawyer stood firm at my side, shaking the men's hands as I waited for whatever the woman was going to say. She stepped up and kissed my cheek, then leaned in to whisper in my ear. "Did you know you can rip a man's scrotum off with the same force you'd throw a punch?" She then pulled back and winked at me before hobbling away.

Okay...that lady was a bit unhinged.

"Bless you both. I wish you a long and happy life together," a couple said, and bowed their heads to us.

The world had gone to shit around us, but people were still paying their respects. It was weird and sweet and...*strange*. When the last person had left, Sawyer sagged against my side. We stood in the grass, covered in water and blood, and he'd finally let go.

'Dad,' he croaked in my head, and my heart tore in two as I reached for him.

My mom and dad sat patiently with Mrs. Hudson at the base of the tree while she wept over Curt's body.

"Why don't you take your mom back home and have her lie down. I'll handle...this." I gestured to the body.

He nodded. "Are you sure?"

There were times in a relationship when one person was hurting more than the other; this was one of those times. Sawyer needed me to step up and I was going to be there for him.

"Yes."

Sawyer walked over to the tree and my mom and dad backed up to give him space. His mother looked up into her son's eyes, swimming with tears, and burst into uncontrollable sobs.

"He's gone," she wailed.

My chest physically ached to watch Sawyer bend down and place one hand on his mother's back and another on his father's chest. Curt's face was covered with my dad's jacket, but you could make out where his chest would be.

"He's with Nana and Papa." Sawyer leaned down and whispered something in his dad's ear that no one could hear but him, and then he picked his mother up into his arms like she was made of glass. She clung to him, wailing uncontrollably, and I wondered if they would need to medicate her somehow. That kind of grief was fucking soul shattering.

My mom and I wiped at our eyes as we watched them walk away, then I called Eugene over.

I had to clear my throat a few times before I could speak without my voice cracking.

"Did he have a will? A desire to be cremated or buried?" I asked Eugene.

The big brute looked absolutely broken; his eyes were vacant and yet he still stood strong. "Yes. Buried. In his family plot."

I nodded. "Can you arrange for a funeral home to prepare his body for burial? Have his personal affects sent to Sawyer?"

We'd need to plan the funeral, but that was something we could deal with tomorrow. He nodded. "Right away."

Then I turned to my parents. "You guys should get home, lock yourselves inside until Sawyer sends word about the next step."

My mom frowned. "Honey, you need us, we can stay—"

I shook myself. "No, I need to know you are safe at home while I help Sawyer. Please. I'll call you later."

They nodded, hugging me, and my mom took one final weepy look at Curt's body and left with my father. I sat down under the tree with my dead father-in-law as guards ran all around us barking orders and dealing with the shit show inside. We had dead and wounded, and even though the fire seemed to be out, the building was still being fully evacuated. It was a nightmare.

I reached out, laying one palm on Curt's chest. "I'm

sorry." My throat tightened as I swallowed back tears. "I'll take care of him for you."

Curt loved Sawyer, jumped in front of a bullet to save him, and I knew he would want to make sure someone was always looking out for him. I didn't know where we went after we died. I wanted to believe in heaven and God and all of that, but blind faith was hard for me. Still, if his soul was lingering somehow, I wanted him to go in peace.

"Can I sit with you?" Sage asked, and I looked up to see her covered in signs of war and holding the present box with my cuffs in them. Blood, soot, and grime marred her beautiful face.

I nodded and she plopped down next to me.

"Thanks for having my back in there," I told her.

She looked offended. "I always have your back." Then she looked over at Curt's body and swallowed hard. "I can't believe…" She shuddered. "My dad's been away on business. He's going to be devastated."

I reached for her hand. "I'm so sorry."

We sat there in silence, guarding the alpha's body from harm until the coroner finally turned up. He looked shaken by the news, eyes wide as he and an assistant unrolled a canvas stretcher. I didn't want to shake him up more, but I wanted to make sure he was going to treat the body properly, with respect.

"Can I trust you with his remains?" I asked, my voice more growly than normal.

The man gulped. "Yes, ma'am. It's my honor to serve the Hudson family in this way. Curt gave me a small business loan five years ago during some rough times."

And now I felt like a dick. "Okay. Thanks. Sorry. I'm—"

I'm in shock and I need therapy.

"It's fine." He smiled sweetly as they hoisted Curt into a body bag and began to zip it closed.

"Wait," I said.

On a whim, I reached out and pulled the silver band from his ring finger and placed it around my thumb, making a mental note to give it to Sawyer's mother later.

Once they were gone and my promise to Sawyer was complete, I turned to Sage.

"I think we should elope. This did not go well." I tried for humor, but it felt wrong in my mouth.

She gave a dry chuckle. "I think you'll—" Sage's phone buzzed, as did mine and everyone's around us.

I turned to look down at the alert on my phone. It was an emergency broadcast similar to an amber alert, but this was from Werewolf City.

The vampires have declared war on Werewolf City. Active duty, reserve members, and anyone over eighteen willing to fight, please report to Sterling Hill campus at 0600 tomorrow morning. From now on, a curfew is in effect. Do not go out after dark.—Sawyer Hudson, Alpha

My eyes widened. War. Like for *real* war?

Sage's spine straightened and Walsh popped out from behind the building, running toward us.

"What does this mean?" I asked.

Were the vampires going to drop bombs on us or something?

"Come on, I'll drive." Walsh ignored my question and tipped his head to Sage and me.

I took one last look at the spot Curt had lain; the grass was smooshed, the blades broken and red from where his body had rested. I knew that I would never be able to look at the base of this tree, or any other probably, and not think of him.

Shaking myself, I ran after Walsh and Sage, and prayed it didn't come to actual war.

CHAPTER THIRTEEN

WALSH DROVE US TO A BIG DADDY MANSION THAT I assumed was his parents' house. It was perched right behind the school and there were a dozen black Range Rovers outside. This must be where Sawyer was.

'*Are you in this giant mansion Walsh just drove me to?*' I asked Sawyer mentally.

'*Yes, love. I asked him to bring you to me. Come inside.*'

We all popped out of the car and Sage and Walsh started to talk to the two guards stationed outside while I stood there like an idiot.

"Step inside, go left, and he's in the office probably. Meet you in there in a sec," Sage told me, and I nodded.

I walked up to the doors, about to knock, and then figured that was stupid since his mom was probably resting and Sawyer had just told me to come in.

The porch was large, lined with a deep oak wood, and I stepped up to the two giant glass doors and turned the handle. Walking inside the travertine lined foyer, I turned left and immediately came face-to-face with Roland. His eyes were red rimmed and glassy like he'd been crying. "Oh, Miss Calloway, it's so good to see you are all right." He pulled me into a hug and my throat tightened as I hugged him back.

Sawyer told me that this man was a member of the family, and I could tell by how sweet he was to me that it held true. "Thank you, Roland." I squeezed him tightly before we both let each other go.

He brushed a few stray tears off of his cheeks and nodded. "Come on in. Mrs. Hudson is resting, but Sawyer has requested you join him in the war room."

War room.

He said war room.

Shit. This was real. This was really happening.

I gulped and walked down the long, dimly lit hall. As we neared, I heard screaming voices. Well, one screaming voice. My fiancé.

"Do I look like I fucking care about money right now? Just do it! I don't care what it costs," Sawyer growled.

Roland opened the door after a light knock, and I stepped inside.

Whoa.

The room was large and completely bare but for a

huge desk made of glass that looked like it was a giant tablet. Around it stood five men. Eugene, Brandon, Quan, some big dude I didn't know with black dreadlocks, and a scrawny secretary dude I'd seen follow his dad around.

"Demi." Sawyer rushed forward and pulled me into his arms. "You okay?" He looked down at me as if assessing me for any wounds he might have missed before. "Shit, our engagement party was ruined. I'm so sorry."

I shook my head. "I don't care."

He nodded. "I know but...I wanted it to be special for you."

His freaking dad died! The last thing on my mind was a special engagement party, but I knew he was a romantic and just wanted me to feel like a queen, and was probably still in shock.

He pulled out a folded piece of paper and slipped it into my back pocket. I frowned.

"I might be up late. Read that later when you're alone," he whispered in my ear.

I just nodded, confused as to why he would write me a note.

"Sir..." Eugene cleared his throat. "With the witches on the bloodsucker's side, our technology will be no match. Tankers, guns, helicopters, they can all be disabled with the flick of the wrist."

Sawyer sighed and I'd never seen him look so old and worn down.

267

He turned to face Eugene. "I know that."

"Are all of the witches against us, or just some?" I asked, assuming Sawyer wanted me in here to share ideas and not just look pretty. Not that I looked very pretty right now covered in blood and ashes.

"Reports are that the large majority wants to side with the vampires. We border Witch Lands, and Queen Drake has promised them our land if they help defeat us in the war," the shrimpy secretary dude said. "And our army is holding the wall at our northern gate for now, but it won't keep. There are more of them than there are us."

Sawyer sighed, pinching the bridge of his nose.

I raised my hand and everyone looked at me. "Why not offer the witches who want to defect a place to live here? Surely we have extra land and housing we could offer to witches willing to fight on our side? Raven said it's pretty bad over there. Everyone can't love it."

Raven's family had been cast out for speaking ill of the high priestess and calling for a public vote of new leadership. The high priestess had been alive for over a thousand years, and so she stayed in power indefinably. Some of the people were ready for change.

If you spoke ill of the high priestess, your electricity would get shut off or your food rationed. They were very controlling of their people.

"Witches come live here? In Werewolf City. Permanently?" Brandon asked, scrunching up his face.

I looked to Sawyer, who was stroking his chin. He

was covered in blood; his hair had flecks of soot in it, and the entire room smelled of smoke. Shit was dire but here he was war planning, trying to save his people from harm. I loved him so much in this moment.

"If we can put aside our...obsession ...with having a certain territory..." Sawyer nodded. "That could work. Pull up the map. Where could we put them?"

The secretary looked like he'd been smacked in the face. "You want me to find an area in Werewolf City to move in *witches*?"

Mr. Dreadlocks growled. "Yes, are you deaf? Your alpha gave you an order, now make it happen."

Sawyer placed a hand on Dreadlocks's shoulder. "It's all right, Commander, it's going to take some getting used to."

Then he looked at me. "Is there a leader of their opposition? Can we get Raven over here to consult with us?"

Holy shit. He was actually listening to my idea. I nodded.

"Tell her I'm sending a car for her and her family," Sawyer told me, and then started barking more orders at other people.

I pulled out my phone and texted my bestie.

Me: Umm so we're at war, the alpha is dead and I need you to come to Werewolf City for a consult... Sawyer is sending a car.

Raven: WTF! Are you okay? Okay...can my parents come?

Me: Yes. Pack for a while. Miss you.

I was hoping to talk Sawyer into letting them stay here long-term, especially if he was letting other witches come.

"Raven and her parents are packing," I told Sawyer.

He nodded, rubbing his face and looking more stressed than I'd ever seen him.

"I think we should—"

A siren went off and a walkie-talkie at the Commanders' belt squawked.

"Vampires have breached the north wall. Orders, sir?" a voice came over the line and my eyes widened.

The Commander looked to Sawyer, who peeled his lips back, his canines lengthening to points and pressing in on his bottom lip. "Kill anything that steps over that wall."

The Commander nodded. "Shoot to kill. I repeat, shoot to kill."

The siren lessened to a low wail and Sawyer paced the room.

"How many in the reserves?" he asked, just as Sage and Walsh walked in.

"Three thousand," The Commander said.

Sawyer stopped dead and spun on his heel. "That's it?"

The Commander swallowed hard. "Your father wasn't keen on war."

Sawyer shook his head. "Well, war is keen on us."

The Commander nodded, his back going rigid. "If I may be relieved sir, I'd like to get to the front line with my men."

Sawyer nodded and the Commander left the room.

Sawyer looked at the scrawny secretary then. "Please check on my mother, make sure the war siren hasn't woken her."

The man nodded and scurried from the room.

"We'll go help at the north wall. Sorry again about your dad." Quan and Brandon both gave Sawyer a quick bro hug and then left. Now it was just Walsh, Sage, Eugene, Sawyer, and I to stare at the map of Magic City that stood open on the tablet. He'd set up an imaginary battle where all of the magical races turned on us, and it didn't look good.

"Someone give me some good fucking news," Sawyer growled, rubbing the bridge of his nose.

Sage pulled out her phone and showed him something. "I've gotten at least a thousand responses from the emergency text you sent out of wolves wanting to enlist," she told her cousin.

"It's not enough! I need at least *ten thousand* more." Sawyer reached up and pulled at his hair.

My eyes flicked to his the moment he said ten thousand.

The Paladins had ten thousand warriors and we'd just done them a favor.

"I know where we can get a couple thousand more warriors," I said boldly.

"No," he growled, as if he could read my thoughts.

Everyone in the room looked confused.

I swallowed hard, stepping up to kiss his cheek. "Sawyer, I can get you thousands more warriors."

He grabbed the sides of my face, peering into my eyes. I saw so much emotion there. Anger, agony, possession. "Not in a million fucking years, Demi," he growled.

"How?" Eugene's voice came from behind me and I stepped back from Sawyer.

"Paladins. They are over ten thousand strong. I can ask for warriors and they will give them to me."

Eugene looked impressed. "Do it. With those kind of numbers we could actually have a chance to win this thing."

Sawyer spun on Eugene. "The Paladin don't have phones and I have an ankle bracelet on. That means she would have to go there alone. *NO.*"

His eyes went yellow and I waited for Eugene to lower his head in submission.

He didn't.

Eugene shouted, "Son, if we don't secure these walls, we are looking at total annihilation within two days, *and* they'll steal your fiancé and drain her blood!"

The veins in Sawyer's neck bulged. "Or they find her on her way to the Paladin lands and just drain her there!"

I cleared my throat. "No one is draining anyone, okay. I can handle myself! I'll go and be right back. I will meet you at the school with thousands more men by morning," I declared.

If I really was the Paladin alpha, then they would come with me and help me out, right?

Sawyer shook his head. "No."

There was a finality in his voice, and I could hear his teeth clamp together and nearly crack as his jaw set.

I sighed. "*Trust me. I'll be right back.*"

He needed to see reason or my parents and everyone we cared about were going to get killed.

"No," he growled again, and this time alpha power lashed into the room wildly.

"We have to put our people first, Sawyer. Before our own needs." I stepped closer to him.

"No." This time it was a whimper. With a sigh, I slipped his dad's ring off my thumb and then I stepped forward and placed it on his ring finger.

"I'm going to be back by morning, with warriors, and we're going to win and get married."

He clamped down on my fingers, a sob forming in his throat.

I didn't want to do this to him. He'd just lost his father and he was vulnerable, but the north gate had already been breached. Soon it would be the east and the south, and what about when the vampires recruited the Ithaki? We were no match for the entirety of Magic City.

I looked to Walsh and Eugene, who'd been watching our passionate display from the sidelines.

They knew what this look was and they both nodded. I nodded back.

They rushed forward and pulled his hands behind him, pinning him back as I stepped away from him. His eyes went wide at the betrayal.

"I'll be right back," I told him, heading for the door. "We're going to win this fucking war."

Then I did the hardest thing I'd ever done. I ran down the hall and left him there screaming my name.

'Not again, don't do this to me again. I can't follow you with the ankle bracelet on!' Sawyer yelled desperately in my head.

'I got this. You have to trust that I am capable without you. I love you and I'm coming right back,' I told him as I reached the front door and burst out into the night.

'Demi, I swear to God if I cannot be there to protect you, I will die from heartbreak. Don't do this to me. I already lost my father. I can't take losing you.'

My chest constricted at his words, but I pressed on.

'I love you. I'll see you in the morning with Paladin warriors. I promise.'

Someone pounded the ground behind me, and I looked back to see Sage.

"You sure?" I asked.

She rolled her eyes. "Bitch, you're not going alone."

With a smile we slipped into the woods of the alpha's property and took off for the border. I knew you couldn't take a car into the Wild Lands; there were no roads.

Sawyer's parents' house was close to the border between the campus and the northeast border wall where the Vampire City coven and the Wild Lands met. I could run vampire-fast, and the sound of cracking bones behind me told me that Sage was shifting to catch up. It was dark out, with the moon high in the sky, and I felt fatigue pull at my muscles as we ran as fast as we could.

Curt was dead.

We were at war.

Sawyer was alpha...early.

So much raced through my mind as Sage and I pounded the ground to the border. It only took about ten minutes to reach the little row of orange flags that demarcated the Wild Lands beyond. A small four-foot cobblestone wall stood there with gaps every twenty or so feet. I could hear yelling and gunfire off in the distance to the north, and I wondered if I could make it to the Paladin and back in time to help.

Sawyer's emotions slammed into me like a tornado; my stomach lurched into my throat as I felt his despair overwhelm me.

"Demi, don't you dare cross that line!" Sawyer's broken voice came from somewhere behind me.

I whimpered in pain as the emotion of leaving him left a gash on my heart a mile wide. Looking over my shoulder, I saw him burst through the trees. I couldn't meet his gaze. He was panting wildly, torso covered in blood and red marks from where Eugene and Walsh had held him. The red blinking light on his ankle bracelet flashed a slow steady rhythm as if reminding us it was there. When I finally looked up into his eyes, they were bright yellow.

"I'm sorry," I whimpered, and backed up into the Wild Lands and behind the markers. Sage followed me over with her tail tucked between her legs.

"Demi!" Sawyer roared. "You don't understand how dangerous this is!" He ran toward me and I backed up farther into the woods, slipping behind the gap in the wall with tears running down my face.

"Sawyer, stop!" I screamed, but he didn't. He ran full speed into the woods, but instead of crossing over the flag line, his entire body seized up and I heard the crack of electricity from where I stood ten feet away. He fell backward, teeth clacking together as he shook on the ground, convulsing.

A sob ripped from my throat at seeing someone I loved in so much agony.

Eugene and Walsh came into the clearing then, panting and taking huge lungfuls of air as they surveyed the scene.

A siren ripped into the night and Sawyer sat up groaning, holding his stomach. He looked at me through the gap in the fence and I paled when his broken blue eyes hit me with utter betrayal.

Eugene thrust a cell phone at Sawyer. "Witches have taken down all of our aerial assault. The eastern wall has fallen. What do we do?"

Fuck.

I backed up a few more steps, knowing now more than ever that we needed the Paladins' help.

Sawyer lowered his head, speaking into the phone, "Put the women and children in the underground bunker and arm every man over seventeen." He hung up and then looked up at me with a haunted expression. "Come home with me now, Demi. Get in the bunker where you will be safe."

That was just the thing. This didn't feel like *home* anymore, nowhere did. And I knew that if I didn't get help, there would be no home to return to.

"I'll be right back. Please forgive me," I managed to say without falling into a blubbering mess. Then I turned my back on the love of my life and ran into the darkness of the Wild Lands.

Sawyer's earsplitting howl, half-human, half-man, split my heart in two and I wondered if our relationship would ever be the same after this.

It had to, right? We were true mates...

ACKNOWLEDGMENTS

A huge thank-you to my editors at Bloom. Christa, Gretchen, and Kylie, you made this baby shine! And to my agents, Flavia and Meire, for always believing in my work. It truly takes a village to get every single book into readers' hands. I have to send out a huge thank-you my readers for buying my books and turning this passion into a career that supports my family. I'm literally living my dream. Thank you to my amazing and supportive family for sharing me with my characters. And lastly, thank you to God for this truly remarkable gift you have given me.

ABOUT THE AUTHOR

Leia Stone is the USA Today bestselling author of multiple bestselling series, including Matefinder, Wolf Girl, The Gilded City, Fallen Academy, and Kings of Avalier. She's sold over three million books, and her Fallen Academy series has been optioned for film. Her novels have been translated into multiple languages and she even dabbles in script writing.

Leia writes urban fantasy and paranormal romance with sassy kick-butt heroines and irresistible love interests. She lives in Spokane, Washington, with her husband and two children.

Instagram: @leiastoneauthor
TikTok: @leiastone
Facebook: leia.stone
Website: www.LeiaStone.com